YORK NOTES

THE GREAT GATSBY

F. SCOTT FITZGERALD

Notes by Julian Cowley

Longman
is an imprint of

PEARSON

York Press

YORK PRESS
322 Old Brompton Road, London SW5 9JH

PEARSON EDUCATION LIMITED
Edinburgh Gate, Harlow,
Essex CM20 2JE, United Kingdom

Associated companies, branches and representatives throughout the world

First published 1998
New edition 2004
This new and fully revised edition 2012

10 9 8 7 6 5 4 3 2 1

ISBN 978–1–4479–1320–7

Illustration on p. 9 by Neil Gower
Phototypeset by Carnegie Book Production
Printed in Slovakia by Neografia

Photo Credits
Martinie/Roger Viollet/Getty Images for page 6 top / © iStockphoto.com/Anton_Sokolov for page 6 middle / 06photo/Shutterstock.com for page 7 / © iStockphoto.com/shunyufan for page 8 / © iStockphoto.com/MmeEmil for page 10 / © iStockphoto.com/anilakduygu for page 11 / © iStockphoto.com/majorosl for page 13 / © iStockphoto.com/psdphotography for page 14 / © iStockphoto.com/Akirastock for page 16 / © iStockphoto.com/senyatkin for page 17 / Balefire/Shutterstock.com for page 19 / © iStockphoto.com/cbarnesphotography for page 20 / © iStockphoto.com/SklepSpozywczy for page 21 / © iStockphoto.com/KeithBinns for page 22 / © iStockphoto.com/aydinmutlu for page 24 / Image Source/Image Source/Getty Images for page 25 / © Radius Images/Alamy for page 26 / © iStockphoto.com/EricHood for page 27 / zhang kan/Shutterstock.com for page 28 / vectorlib-com/Shutterstock.com for page 30 / © iStockphoto.com/AdrlnJunkie for page 31 / © iStockphoto.com/lebanmax for page 32 / © iStockphoto.com/AndyL for page 33 / © iStockphoto.com/Bluberries for page 34 / Tyler Olson/Shutterstock.com for page 35 / Dundanim/Shutterstock.com for page 36 / © iStockphoto.com/THEPALMER for page 37 / © iStockphoto.com/MikeyLPT for page 38 / © iStockphoto.com/northlightimages for page 39 / © iStockphoto.com/dem10 for page 40 / © iStockphoto.com/okeyphotos for page 42 / Zinaida/Shutterstock.com for page 44 / Roman Sigaev/Shutterstock.com for page 45 / © iStockphoto.com/caracterdesign for page 46 / © iStockphoto.com/sbrogan for page 48 / © iStockphoto.com/mammuth for page 49 / Monkey Business Images/Shutterstock.com for page 50 / © iStockphoto.com/annedde for page 51 / © iStockphoto.com/RelaxFoto.de for page 52 / © iStockphoto.com/AndreyPopov for page 53 / © iStockphoto.com/Tashka for page 54 / © iStockphoto.com/Jitalia17 for page 56 / © iStockphoto.com/scanrail for page 58 / Cosma/Shutterstock.com for page 59 / Brian A Jackson/Shutterstock.com for page 61 / Fer Gregory/Shutterstock.com for page 64 / © iStockphoto.com/robynmac for page 65 / © iStockphoto.com/egeeksen for page 66 / © iStockphoto.com/wragg for page 67 / Christian Delbert/Shutterstock.com for page 68 / © iStockphoto.com/sumnersgraphicsinc for page 69 / Brian A Jackson/Shutterstock.com for page 70 / © iStockphoto.com/dem10 for page 71 / Cedric Weber/Shutterstock.com for page 72 / kavram/Shutterstock.com for page 73 / © iStockphoto.com/Goldfaery for page 89 / © iStockphoto.com/skynesher for page 91

CONTENTS

PART FOUR: STRUCTURE, FORM AND LANGUAGE

PART FIVE: CONTEXTS AND CRITICAL DEBATES

PART SIX: GRADE BOOSTER

ESSENTIAL STUDY TOOLS

PART ONE: INTRODUCING *THE GREAT GATSBY*

HOW TO STUDY *THE GREAT GATSBY*

These Notes can be used in a range of ways to help you read, study and (where relevant) revise for your exam or assessment.

READING THE NOVEL

Read the novel once, fairly quickly, for pleasure. This will give you a good sense of the over-arching shape of the **narrative**, and a good feel for the highs and lows of the action, the pace and tone, and the sequence in which information is withheld or revealed. You could ask yourself:

- How do individual characters change or develop? How do my own responses to them change?
- From whose **point of view** is the novel told? Does this change or remain the same?
- Are the events presented chronologically, or is the time scheme altered in some way?
- What impressions do the locations and settings, such as West Egg, make on my reading and response to the text?
- What sort of language, style and form am I aware of as the novel progresses? Does Fitzgerald paint detail precisely, or is there deliberate vagueness or ambiguity – or both? Does he use imagery, or recurring motifs and symbols?

On your second reading, make detailed notes around the key areas highlighted above and in the Assessment Objectives, such as form, language, structure (AO2), links and connections to other texts (AO3) and the context/background for the novel (AO4). These may seem quite demanding, but these Notes will suggest particular elements to explore or jot down.

> **CONTEXT** **A04**
>
> Fitzgerald decided to call his novel *The Great Gatsby* shortly before it was published. Titles he had earlier considered included *Trimalchio in West Egg* and *Under the Red, White, and Blue*. It is useful to think about how the title he eventually chose focuses your attention as you read and interpret the novel.

INTERPRETING OR CRITIQUING THE NOVEL

Although it's not helpful to think in terms of the novel being 'good' or 'bad', you should consider the different ways the novel can be read. How have critics responded to it? Do their views match yours – or do you take a different viewpoint? Are there different ways you can interpret specific events, characters or settings? This is a key aspect in AO3, and it can be helpful to keep a log of your responses and the various perspectives which are expressed both by established critics and by classmates, your teacher, or other readers.

REFERENCES AND SOURCES

You will be expected to draw on critics' comments, or refer to source information from the period or the present. Make sure you make accurate, clear notes of writers or sources you have used – for example, noting down titles of works, authors' names, website addresses, dates, etc. You may not have to reference all these things when you respond to a text, but knowing the source of your information will allow you to go back to it, if need be – and to check its accuracy and relevance.

REVISING FOR AND RESPONDING TO AN ASSESSED TASK OR EXAM QUESTION

The structure and the contents of these Notes are designed to help give you the relevant information or ideas you need to answer tasks you have been set. First, work out the key words or ideas from the task (for example, 'form', 'Chapter 3', 'Daisy'), then read the relevant parts of the Notes that relate to these terms or words, selecting what is useful for revision or written response. Then, turn to **Part Six: Grade Booster** for help in formulating your actual response.

THE GREAT GATSBY IN CONTEXT

F. SCOTT FITZGERALD: LIFE AND TIMES

CONTEXT A04

The Great Gatsby was actually completed while the Fitzgeralds were living in the South of France. They found it cheaper to live there than in New York City. Note that the couple had met while he was stationed at an Army training camp in Alabama. Their meeting is clearly reflected in the circumstances of Gatsby's first encounter with Daisy.

1896	(24 September) Francis Scott Fitzgerald is born into a middle-class family in St Paul, Minnesota
1917	(April) America enters the First World War
1918	(June) Fitzgerald is posted for army training to Camp Sheridan, near Montgomery, Alabama; while there he meets and falls in love with society 'golden girl' Zelda Sayre
1919	The outcome of the baseball World Series is fixed, with the involvement of New York gangster Arnold Rothstein
1920	Fitzgerald marries Zelda Sayre in New York; his first novel, *This Side of Paradise*, is published

1920	A Prohibition law is introduced in America, making manufacture, transportation and sale of alcoholic drink illegal; it remains in force until 1933
1924	F. Scott and Zelda Fitzgerald move to the South of France, where he works on *The Great Gatsby*
1925	(April) *The Great Gatsby* is published in New York
1929	The Wall Street Crash ushers in the Great Depression, a decade-long financial crisis that causes much hardship for working-class Americans
1940	(21 December) Fitzgerald dies in Hollywood, California

A STORY OF THE WEST?

CHECK THE FILM A04

The Great Gatsby appeared at a time when the popularity of cinema was really starting to take off. A silent film based upon the book was actually filmed in 1926. Another attempt was made in 1949, a black-and-white talkie with the title role taken by actor Alan Ladd. A glamorous 1979 version had Robert Redford as Gatsby and Mia Farrow playing Daisy. The latest adaptation, directed by Baz Luhrman, and featuring Leonardo DiCaprio and Carey Mulligan in the key roles, is scheduled for release at the end of 2012.

Like the main characters in *The Great Gatsby*, F. Scott Fitzgerald was born in the American Midwest. His family were moderately wealthy Irish-American and Roman Catholic. He attended Princeton University in New Jersey, a rival in prestige to Yale and Harvard, but was always conscious that many of his classmates came from well-established families and more wealthy backgrounds. At the end of his life, Fitzgerald lived in Hollywood, on the west coast of America, writing scripts for films in order to make money.

THE INTERNATIONAL THEME

The Great Gatsby is a novel about being American; indeed, at the time of its publication Fitzgerald wanted the book to be called *Under the Red, White, and Blue*, alluding to the national flag, the Stars and Stripes. But he understood that America's identity involved certain attitudes to Europe; it has been a complex relationship, and that is reflected in the novel.

THE JAZZ AGE

Fitzgerald is regarded as the leading chronicler of the Jazz Age. In his novels and short stories, he captured the pleasure-seeking lifestyle of the 1920s in America. This pursuit of pleasure was in part a reaction to the First World War, which seemed to mark the end of an old era. The world was changing, getting faster. There were more and more cars on the roads, telephones allowed instant communication across large distances, and human beings had started to fly in aeroplanes. Electric lighting made homes and public spaces brighter, gramophones turned people's rooms into dance halls, magazines spread gossip about celebrities and moving images of life were projected onto the cinema's silver screen.

Jazz music provided the soundtrack for this new way of life, especially in a modern city such as New York. It was music for young people to dance to and party. Some African-American musicians of the time, such as Louis Armstrong, Bessie Smith, Jelly Roll Morton and Duke Ellington were great artists and their music has endured. But the dance music in *The Great Gatsby* seems to have been disconnected from its African-American origins. The novel shows America in the Jazz Age divided along lines of race as well as class and gender.

FLAPPERS

The name 'flappers' was applied during the 1920s to young women who lived far more liberated lives than their mothers or grandmothers. Flappers often had their hair cut in a short, boyish bob, and raised the hemlines of their skirts a lot higher than the previous generation would have dared. They wore more make-up and would dance, drink, smoke and drive in a way that some older Americans considered indecent. The emphasis was essentially on greater freedom of movement and behaviour.

A number of Fitzgerald's short stories feature these young and high-spirited flappers. Perhaps the figure closest to a flapper in *The Great Gatsby* is Miss Baedeker, the drunken young woman who tries to slump against Nick's shoulder at Gatsby's party in Chapter 6. Jordan Baker doesn't fit into the flapper category but she is, nonetheless, thoroughly modern – independent, a celebrity sportswoman, and yet sceptical about everything.

PROHIBITION AND ORGANISED CRIME

Between 1920 and 1933 the manufacture, transportation and sale of alcohol in America was prohibited by law. It was not illegal to drink it, but the law was designed to stop people having access to it. Jay Gatsby is said to have made money from bootlegging, the illicit supply of alcohol, and despite the ban drunkenness is common in this novel.

In Chapter 4 we see how close he actually is to the crooked gambler Meyer Wolfshiem. During the 1920s, American cities such as New York and Chicago witnessed a great deal of violence as rival gangsters competed for power and influence. Legendary figures such as Al Capone, 'Lucky' Luciano, Meyer Lansky and Dutch Schultz were major players in the criminal underworld.

It was notable that a high percentage of these gangsters were from families who had arrived fairly recently in America – individuals who grew up in energetic Italian, Irish and Jewish communities, and then found that respectable routes to success were denied to them because their backgrounds were so different from that of people such as Tom Buchanan.

CHECK THE BOOK `A04`

Fitzgerald's novels portray the 1920s in a far more sombre light than his short stories, which were written for magazine publication and mostly lack the serious concerns of the longer works. The stories have been conveniently collected in the volume *Flappers and Philosophers* (Penguin Books, 2010).

CONTEXT `A04`

Note that women were not granted the vote in all states of America until August 1920. America remained a patriarchal, male-dominated society.

CONTEXT `A04`

A sad footnote is that Fitzgerald was addicted to alcohol; this undoubtedly contributed to his death at the early age of forty-four.

STUDY FOCUS: KEY ISSUES A02

Key issues of *The Great Gatsby* are:

- The character and fate of Jay Gatsby as a reflection of the character and fate of America
- The relationship between the New World (America) and the Old World (Europe)
- The relationship between the present and the past
- The loss of innocence and the capacity to feel wonder
- The reliability of Nick as a **narrator**
- The relationship between **point of view** and truth, or between belief and understanding
- The nature of memory
- The worth of Daisy as the object of Gatsby's love
- The value of hope and dreams in an age of cynicism and materialism
- The value of writing.

Keep these ideas in mind as you read through the novel. You may be examined on one or a combination of these important issues.

SETTING

The action of *The Great Gatsby* takes place in New York, the major city on America's East coast. Nick Carraway works in the financial district, centred on Wall Street, in the Lower Manhattan district. Nick is a commuter and lives on the North Shore of Long Island, an actual island but still part of the New York metropolitan area.

Fitzgerald called the village where Nick and Gatsby live West Egg; the Buchanans live in East Egg. West Egg is based upon an actual place called King's Point, on the Great Neck peninsula; East Egg is based upon Sands Point, a village on the Cow Neck Peninsula. These two peninsulas jut into a stretch of water called Long Island Sound, which is an estuary of the Atlantic Ocean. New York's East River runs into Long Island Sound.

George and Myrtle Wilson's home is in a 'valley of ashes' (p. 26) that seems to be based upon the Corona Ash Dumps, refuse tips for the city's waste, formerly located on the site of what is now a public park called Flushing Meadows.

CONTEXT A04

Flushing Meadows park, in the New York district called Queens, now contains the venue for the US Open tennis tournament.

LOCATIONS IN THE NOVEL

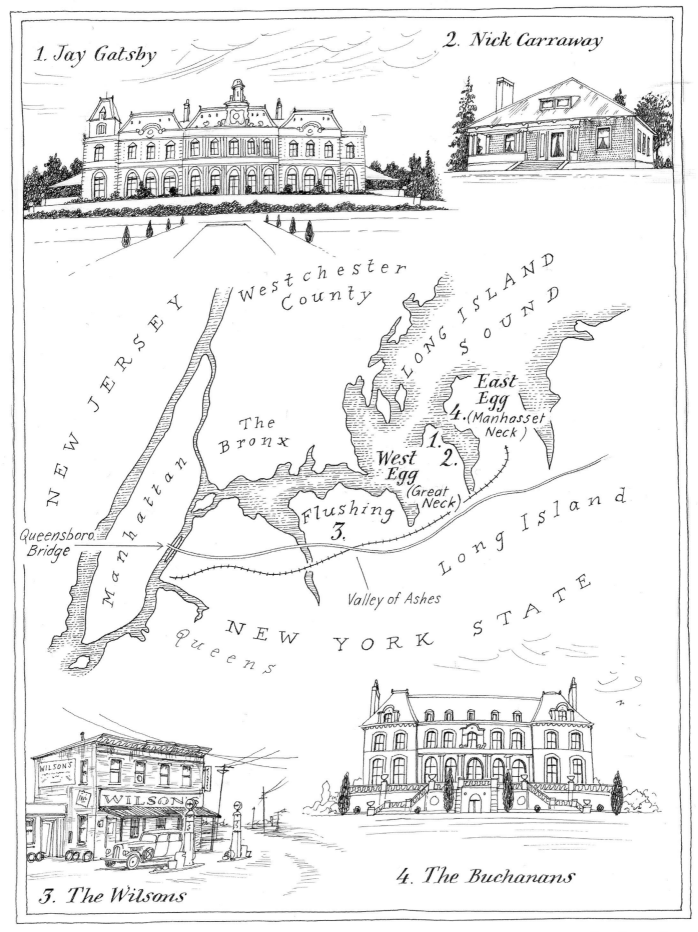

1. Jay Gatsby

2. Nick Carraway

3. The Wilsons

4. The Buchanans

SYNOPSIS

NICK CARRAWAY NARRATES

In 1924, Nick Carraway, from the Midwest of the United States, writes an account of certain experiences which affected him deeply while he was working as a bondsman in the New York financial world, a few years earlier. The key events centre upon his next-door neighbour – the glamorous, wealthy and mysterious Jay Gatsby, who is renowned for hosting extravagant parties at his mansion in West Egg village on Long Island.

THE BUCHANANS

Nick visits Daisy Buchanan, a distant relative, and her very rich husband, Tom, whom he had known at university. At their house in East Egg village he meets a young woman named Jordan Baker, who was Daisy's bridesmaid and is now a well-known golfer. Nick and Jordan develop a friendship, which at times has romantic overtones. At one of Gatsby's flamboyant parties, Nick learns from Jordan that Daisy and Gatsby were once in love. They were separated when Gatsby – like Nick himself – was sent to Europe, as a soldier, during the First World War. During his absence overseas, Daisy met and married Tom Buchanan. The Buchanans have a young daughter, Pammy. Jordan also tells Nick that Tom is having an extra-marital affair.

GATSBY AND DAISY

Five years after their brief love affair, Jay Gatsby remains infatuated with Daisy. He now lives across the bay from her house, and his parties are staged in the hope that they will attract her attention. He wants to win back her love. At Gatsby's instigation, Nick invites Daisy to have tea with him. Gatsby is there too, and he and Daisy are reunited. For a brief period their love seems to flicker back to life. Meanwhile, Tom has introduced Nick to his mistress, Myrtle Wilson, whose husband, George, runs a garage in a bleak district, midway between the city and West Egg.

TOM AND MYRTLE

Nick visits an apartment in the city that Tom keeps for his affair with Myrtle. The three of them are joined by Myrtle's sister Catherine and a couple called McKee, who live in the flat below. They talk and drink whisky. Myrtle expresses contempt for her husband George, and recalls how impressed she was by Tom's expensive clothes when they first met on a train. Myrtle insists on repeating Daisy's name when she is drunk. In response, Tom breaks her nose.

GATSBY THE BOOTLEGGER

Nick is intrigued by Gatsby's lifestyle, but disturbed by sinister rumours about his mysterious past. He is said by some to have killed a man; others say he was a German spy during the First World War. The truth emerges that Gatsby has changed his name from James Gatz. He grew up in the Midwest, where his parents unsuccessfully ran a farm. He left home and spent five years travelling with a wealthy prospector named Dan Cody before joining the army and rising to the rank of major. After the First World War, Gatsby moved to the East coast and established contacts in the criminal underworld. Over lunch one day, Gatsby introduces Nick to his friend Meyer Wolfshiem, a criminal who fixed the outcome of the 1919 World Series baseball tournament. It seems that Gatsby, with Wolfshiem's help, became rich through bootlegging, the unlawful distribution of alcoholic drink – which was prohibited in America during the 1920s. Tom challenges him with this accusation when the two meet at a drinking party at the Plaza Hotel, in New York's Manhattan district.

THE DEATH OF MYRTLE WILSON

After the party at the Plaza, Daisy and Gatsby drive back to Long Island in his car. Earlier that day, George Wilson had told Tom Buchanan that he and his wife Myrtle were planning to move to the West and make a fresh start. Tom was shocked by this news. As Gatsby's car approaches the garage, Myrtle, who has been arguing with her husband, sees the vehicle and mistakenly believes that Tom Buchanan is driving it. She runs into the road, intending to speak with him but is hit and killed. The car fails to stop. There are witnesses to the incident, including the Wilsons' neighbour, Michaelis. Nick, Tom and Jordan, following in another vehicle, stop at the scene and learn of Myrtle's death. Later, Gatsby tells Nick that he intends to take the blame for the accident, even though Daisy was at the wheel.

THE DEATH OF JAY GATSBY

Next day, George Wilson, deranged following the death of Myrtle, shoots and kills Gatsby, who is floating on an inflatable mattress in his swimming pool. Wilson then commits suicide. Nick makes all the arrangements for Gatsby's funeral. It is virtually unattended. The Buchanans have left New York. Meyer Wolfshiem says he is unable to attend. Gatsby's father, Henry C. Gatz arrives from the Midwest, proud (though sadly mistaken) that his son has achieved so much through cleverness and hard work.

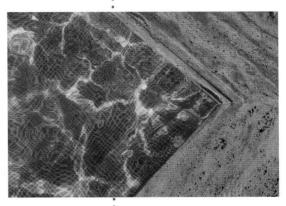

NICK RETURNS TO THE MIDWEST

Nick decides to return to the Midwest, where he writes this story, but before leaving the city he meets Tom Buchanan on the street, by chance. Tom admits he told George Wilson that Gatsby was driving the car which killed Myrtle. The novel ends with Nick contemplating Gatsby's house in the darkness, musing on the significance of Gatsby's dedication to his dream, and on the harsh reality which led to his destruction.

STUDY FOCUS: MODERNISM   A04

During the early twentieth century, new styles appeared in literature, as in other arts, that became known as modernism. Literary modernism tended to deal with topics that were controversial and also to experiment with new forms and techniques that often posed a real challenge to readers.

F. Scott Fitzgerald was not an experimental modernist, but he was self-conscious about language and form, and was aware of advances in **narrative** technique made by early modernists such as Henry James (1843–1916) and Joseph Conrad (1857–1924), both of whom he greatly admired.

CONTEXT   A04

The American writer Gertrude Stein (1874–1946) and the Irish novelist James Joyce (1882–1941) both produced modernist work that many readers still find difficult.

CHAPTER 1

SUMMARY

- It is 1924. Nick Carraway has returned to the Midwest and is writing a book about events that occurred a couple of years earlier, when he was living on Long Island, New York, in a suburban 'village' (p. 9) called West Egg.
- Nick begins his narration with some self-analysis, trying to pin down aspects of his own character. He also provides a few details about his background. Nick's father runs a family hardware business. Nick himself was sent to France, as a soldier, during the First World War (1914–18).
- Jay Gatsby, Nick's neighbour on West Egg, lives in a mansion. It is a wealthy area. Nick refers to 'the consoling proximity of millionaires', and describes buildings in nearby East Egg as 'white palaces' (p. 11).
- Nick tells of a visit to the house of Tom Buchanan, an acquaintance from Yale University. Tom's wife, Daisy, is Nick's second cousin once removed. Tom Buchanan is physically powerful and extremely rich.
- Nick meets Daisy's friend Jordan Baker, who is a well-known golfer.
- Tom makes racist comments, drawing support for his views from a recently published book, Goddard's *The Rise of the Coloured Empires*.
- Jordan tells Nick that Tom is having an affair with 'some woman in New York' (p. 20). This woman – later we learn that her name is Myrtle Wilson – calls Tom, on the telephone, during dinner.
- Later, in the moonlight, Nick catches his first glimpse of Gatsby, who seems to be captivated by a green electric light shining from the end of the Buchanans' private dock.

GRADE BOOSTER   A04

To get the best grades at AS and A2, you need to have an excellent understanding of the contexts that lie behind a text. On a superficial level you could say that *The Great Gatsby* is a love story, or simply about friendship or ambition. It is the historical and cultural context that make it such a complex work. Some knowledge and understanding of these is key to achieving an A or A*.

ANALYSIS

NEW BEGINNINGS

Right at the start of his narration Nick talks about advice he received from his father. Jay Gatsby, we later find out, has turned his back on his parents and has found a very different role model in Dan Cody, his 'mentor'. An important theme in *The Great Gatsby* is the relationship of the past to the present, including what is handed on from one generation to the next. This may take the form of material wealth, but it may also be a set of values, attitudes, or expectations.

We can compare Gatsby's personal history with the history of the American republic, which declared its independence from British rule in 1776. America was asserting itself as a New World, no longer governed by Old World assumptions. America came into existence as a land where anything is possible, and the past is not allowed to set limits.

For a long time, the American West was seen as a place where there was empty space, a kind of blank sheet that Americans could use to start their individual life stories again from scratch. The American West became synonymous with the possibility of a new beginning. Note that both Nick and Gatsby live in West Egg village. The village is geographically located on America's East coast, on Long Island, New York. But the word 'West' links Nick and Gatsby to a widely held belief that life in America is all about hope and possibility. Note that the name 'Egg' seems an additional promise of new life. In the sunshine, on West Egg, Nick has 'that familiar conviction that life was beginning over again with the summer' (p. 10). But the twin Eggs are no more than rocky promontories jutting into Long Island Sound.

CONTEXT   A04

On 4 July 1776, the Declaration of Independence proclaimed that the American colonies were no longer part of the British Empire. The Declaration famously asserted: 'We hold these truths to be self-evident, that all men are created equal, that they are endowed by their Creator with certain unalienable Rights, that among these are Life, Liberty and the pursuit of Happiness'.

STUDY FOCUS: THE NARRATOR

A02

Nick Carraway, as the narrator, takes the reader into his confidence. He is sharing with us his recollection of certain experiences. At the same time, telling the story, in his own way, is helping him to come to terms with those experiences. Narration helps Nick to understand the significance of events. You will notice immediately that his style can be challenging. Nick's sentences can be grammatically complex, and his vocabulary is at times unfamiliar and even obscure.

Nick is a character in the novel as well as its **narrator**, and the first person he analyses is himself. His narration is not neutral. Aspects of his character are reflected in the information he offers us, and in the way he presents it. As we read *The Great Gatsby*, we need to be aware of what is being revealed about Nick as well as grasping what he tells us about the other characters.

WAR AND PEACE

Nick's great-uncle avoided fighting in the American Civil War (1861–5), and managed to build up a thriving business.

Nick and Gatsby, on the other hand, served in the First World War in Europe, after America had joined the conflict in 1917. Gatsby was promoted to the rank of major, an advance in social status that enabled him to make useful connections on the way to getting rich.

But one of America's earliest ambitions was to remain a peaceful nation, to avoid war. In that respect it had clearly failed.

READING NICK CARRAWAY

Note that although the First World War ended in 1918, Nick's move to the East did not occur until 1922. This may reflect the fact that he is not by nature an impulsive person, but it might also suggest that other factors were involved in his decision to move. Perhaps his difficult love affair back home played a larger part than he is willing to admit.

Nick does not present himself as a passionate man, but his imaginative writing style does not seem to match the outlook of a matter-of-fact worker in finance. We may conclude that there are emotional depths to Nick's character that do not feature in the way he openly portrays himself. We should ask why Nick is so fascinated by Jay Gatsby that he chooses to tell his story.

NEW WORLD WEALTH, OLD WORLD STATUS

Nick mentions a belief in the Carraway family that they are descended from the Buccleuchs, upper-class British landowners. In fact, Nick's family runs an unglamorous hardware business selling practical items. In *The Great Gatsby*, we see that despite the Declaration of Independence and the real horrors of the recent war, Europe still attracts wealthy Americans.

Items imported from Europe are an indication of social status. There is much discussion of Gatsby's Oxford education, his Rolls-Royce car, his mansion based on a French model and his shirts sent from London. The Buchanans have spent a year in France, not on war service (like Gatsby and Nick), but seeking pleasure. Tom and Daisy's palatial house has a series of French windows and an Italian sunken garden. All these details help to construct an image that seems closer to old-fashioned European aristocratic values than to modern America's democratic ideal.

CHECK THE BOOK A04

Fitzgerald's friend Ernest Hemingway wrote *The Sun Also Rises* (1926), a novel about uprooted Americans drifting aimlessly in Europe after the First World War. Such figures came to be known as the Lost Generation. The Buchanans, in *The Great Gatsby*, are depicted as wealthy drifters.

Note, however, that these wealthy characters live in a distinctively twentieth-century American technological environment. In the 1920s, it was a relatively new world of cars, motorboats, telephones, cinema and electric lighting.

WHAT'S IN A NAME?

Daisy's name evokes a delicate white flower. Nick actually remarks that Daisy opens up 'in a flower-like way' (p. 24). Is this **simile** convincing? Daisy's life seems to be led in an entirely artificial world of wealth and luxury. She seems far removed from the natural world.

Myrtle, who appears in the next chapter, also has a plant's name. In contrast to the delicate daisy, the myrtle is a rather hardy shrub. This plant name seems to suit the tough conditions of Myrtle Wilson's life. But note that in Mediterranean cultures, myrtle has been associated with love; in the ancient world, myrtle was considered to be sacred to Venus, the goddess of love. Myrtle is, of course, Tom Buchanan's mistress.

Note that Carraway, when spelt 'caraway', is the name of a tall, yellowish plant with thin leaves and seeds that are widely used in cooking. Does this detail tell us anything about Nick? The homely name Carraway certainly seems to place him at a distance from the upper-class dukes of Buccleuch. Buchanan, on the other hand, is actually the name of a Scottish clan who own land near Loch Lomond, in Stirlingshire.

RACIAL ISSUES

Tom Buchanan's racist comments, bolstered by reference to a recently published book, suggest that America in the 1920s was divided along racial lines, as well as those of social class and gender. American history has often been marked by prejudice and conflict between groups with different cultural or racial backgrounds.

Tom Buchanan considers his own northern European ancestry to be a sure indication of his superiority to people from other backgrounds, especially African Americans, many of whose ancestors were taken by force to work as slaves in the New World. Between the end of the Civil War, in 1865, and the action of this novel, in 1922, many African Americans had moved from the rural South to the major cities of the northern states in search of a new life. The vast majority remained poor and underprivileged.

CRITICAL VIEWPOINT A03

In his description of Gatsby's mansion, surrounded by a vast lawn and garden, Nick mentions 'a marble swimming pool' (p. 11). At this point in the **narrative** the pool is a detail that adds to our sense of Gatsby's wealth. But by the end of the novel it takes on more sinister significance, as the location of his death.

CONTEXT A04

In 1861, civil war broke out between America's slaveholding southern states, known as the Confederacy, and the more industrial northern states, known as the Union. It lasted four years and resulted in the abolition of slavery. But the experience of Americans fighting amongst themselves was deeply damaging to the young nation's image. Over 600,000 soldiers died and it was one of the first conflicts to use mass-produced weapons.

REVISION FOCUS: TASK 1   A02

How far do you agree with the statements below?

- Nick Carraway is an unreliable narrator.
- In *The Great Gatsby* America is portrayed as a society in love with the European past.

Try writing opening paragraphs for essays based on the discussion points above. Set out your arguments clearly.

GLOSSARY

10   **Midas and Morgan and Maecenas** in Greek mythology, Midas, a king, wished that whatever he touched would turn to gold. His wish was granted by the god Dionysus, but it soon became clear that this apparent blessing was actually a curse.

John Pierpont Morgan (1837–1913) was an extremely wealthy American financier and art collector. Gaius Maecenas (*c.*70–8 BC) was a Roman politician and generous supporter of the arts

GLOSSARY

10 **the egg in the Columbus story** it was suggested to Christopher Columbus (1451–1506) that another explorer would have discovered America if he had not done so. In response, Columbus issued a challenge to make an egg stand upright. Only he managed to do so – by flattening one end. His point was that although this was possible for others, it was he who found the way

11 **one of the most powerful ends** an 'end', in American football, is the player at the end of the line, facing the opposition. He needs to be a good sprinter

Lake Forest affluent northern suburb of Chicago

12 **Georgian Colonial mansion** an eighteenth-century building. In 1776, America broke away from colonial rule by Britain's King George III

18 *The Rise of the Coloured Empires* **by this man Goddard** a thinly veiled reference to *The Rising Tide of Color Against White World Supremacy*, published in 1920 by the American historian and journalist Lothrop Stoddard

20 **a nightingale come over on the Cunard or White Star Line** the nightingale, a bird famously celebrated by the Romantic poet John Keats, is not found in America, so Daisy imagines that one has travelled the Atlantic on a British ocean liner

22 *Saturday Evening Post* a widely read magazine, to which Fitzgerald was a regular and well-paid contributor

23 **Westchester** an exclusive northern suburb of New York City

24 **Louisville** a long-established city in Kentucky, named after the French king Louis XVI (1754–93)

CONTEXT A04

America has a Latin motto, *e pluribus unum*, meaning 'one from many'. It was chosen in 1776 to indicate that what had formerly been thirteen separate colonies would now combine to form a single republic. Over time this motto has deepened in significance as the population of America has grown through waves of immigration. 'One from many' now suggests a nation made up of people whose origins lie in many other countries and cultures.

KEY QUOTATIONS: CHAPTER 1   A01

Key quotation 1: In describing Gatsby, Nick says he is drawn to him because of his 'extraordinary gift for hope' (p. 8).

Possible interpretations:

- Points to an underlying hopefulness in Nick's own character.
- Connects with the wider context of the 'American Dream', in which anything seems to be possible.
- Sets Gatsby apart from the cynicism and world-weariness of other characters.

Key quotation 2: During dinner, Tom bursts out 'violently' with the comment 'Civilisation's going to pieces' (p. 18).

Possible interpretations:

- Conveys Tom's forcefulness, and also his violent nature.
- Sets the scene in the cultural context of race relations in 1920s America.
- Provides a strong contrast between Tom's gloomy pessimism and Gatsby's optimism.

Other useful quotations:

- Nick on West Egg society: 'the consoling proximity of millionaires' (p. 11)
- On Gatsby: 'his heightened sensitivity to the promises of life' (p. 8)
- On Daisy and Jordan's chatter: 'as cool as their white dresses and their impersonal eyes' (p. 17)
- Tom on race: 'It's up to us, who are the dominant race, to watch out or these other races will have control of things' (p. 18)

EXTENDED COMMENTARY

CHAPTER 1, PP. 17–18

Reading this passage in isolation, it is easy to forget the important fact that *The Great Gatsby* is first of all a book about a man writing a book. We are not witnessing this scene at first hand, although it may seem on the surface that we are. Nick Carraway is re-creating events for us, filtering them through his own personal sense of their significance.

Fitzgerald, the author behind Nick's account, is presenting a scene, set in the Buchanans' house, that involves dramatic **dialogue** between the characters. Such dialogue is an effective means of varying the tone, by introducing the sound of different voices into the narration.

In this way, Fitzgerald prevents Nick's own voice from seeming monotonous or too self-absorbed. Other voices enhance our sense of the characters, and help to develop the storyline. This scene seems complete in itself, but words and actions found here echo and **foreshadow** other words and actions in *The Great Gatsby*. This patterning of the **narrative**, which is often intricate and subtle, creates threads of meaning that result in a rich and complex reading experience, despite the fact that it is not a long novel (see **Part Four: Structure**).

Nick makes reference to Miss Baker. This is the first time he and Jordan have met, so there is a degree of formality. Soon, however, Nick will be calling her by her first name, and before long he will be kissing her. Nick's relationship with Jordan develops in a way

that may surprise us, given what he has told us about his reserved character. Can we trust Nick? We learn later that he was still sending letters, at this point, to a girl he had left in the Midwest. We need to watch Nick's character carefully and not simply accept what he tells us.

Jordan and Daisy discuss making a plan, but Jordan is yawning, and Daisy is at a loss, unable to envisage a future that is different from the present. Fitzgerald is portraying the lives of these rich Americans as directionless. They merely drift, feeling that life holds no further possibilities for them. They seem to embody the very opposite of the hopefulness Nick says he values.

Nick notes 'the absence of all desire' (p. 17) in the conversation between Jordan and Daisy. They do not really express or communicate anything, but engage in inconsequential banter. These wealthy women seem to have all they need. Yet their lives lack purpose.

Their eyes are said to appear 'impersonal' (p. 17), no more expressive than their conversation. Eyes, sight and vision form an important thematic thread running through *The Great Gatsby*. At the beginning of the next chapter, those 'impersonal eyes' find an echo in the huge blank stare of Doctor T. J. Eckleburg's advertising hoarding.

Instead of looking to the future, Daisy focuses upon her injured finger. It could be argued that she is essentially a passive figure; things happen to her, and she is content to be shaped by events and other people, rather than controlling her own destiny. She looks at the bruised finger 'with an awed expression' (p. 17). The adjective 'awed' seems entirely inappropriate to this trivial injury. This suggests a lack of proportion in Daisy's judgement, and in her responses. She seems to see life in an exaggerated, distorted fashion. At the same time, the word 'awed' is an example of Fitzgerald's careful verbal patterning; it anticipates the sense of wonder at the heart of Gatsby's enchanted vision.

Daisy's finger has been hurt by her physically powerful husband Tom, although she says it was an accident. The novel contains several other accidents, and numerous allusions to the role of accidental occurrences in human life. This small injury **foreshadows** a far more disturbing incident in the next chapter, where Tom deliberately breaks the nose of his mistress, Myrtle Wilson, when she drunkenly insists on repeating Daisy's name. Here, Daisy upsets Tom by repeating the word 'hulking'. That parallel in the action strengthens the foreshadowing of Myrtle's injury.

Nick interrupts the dialogue with a brief comment on the distinction between social manners in the American East and the West. Significantly, he says that dinner parties in the East are predictable and drift to an inevitable conclusion, whereas those in the West have plenty of nervous energy, which may result in uncomfortable situations, but at least they have life. Each phase of the Western dinner party is a surge into the uncertain future.

It may seem strange to talk in this way about a meal, but Nick is building a distinction that runs throughout the novel between the hopeful, forward-looking, energetic West and the bored East, trapped in routine and drifting aimlessly.

Note how Nick assumes the role of the unsophisticated rural Midwesterner, asking whether they can talk about crops instead, as that would make him feel more at home. Of course, he has been educated at Yale University (see photo), and his casual remarks about the claret – red wine from Bordeaux in France – are a sign of his actual sophistication. Nick often lays claim to a simplicity of character that is clearly at odds with the life he has in fact led.

Tom Buchanan, like Nick, attended Yale. But his racist outburst indicates a kind of ignorance and coarseness. The manner, as well as the content, of his speech conveys a bullying quality, plus a basic lack of intelligence which clashes with his arrogant air of social superiority. In the course of the novel, we discover that Tom has repeatedly committed adultery since he married Daisy. We might ask why Daisy agreed to become this man's wife. Was his wealth the main attraction? Or his physical power? Is Daisy a passive person who merely does what she is told to do?

Daisy and Jordan are dressed in white. Colour symbolism contributes to the narrative patterning of *The Great Gatsby*, and whiteness is one of its principal threads. At times Fitzgerald uses its conventional connotations of purity and innocence, but here 'whiteness' takes on a sinister resonance as the bigoted Tom violently proclaims a need to defend the perceived superiority of the white race.

CHAPTER 2

SUMMARY

- Nick describes a 'valley of ashes' (p. 26), a bleak area between New York City and the suburban village of West Egg. It is watched over by the huge bespectacled eyes of an optician's advertising hoarding.
- Nick is introduced to Tom Buchanan's mistress, Myrtle, the wife of George Wilson, a garage mechanic.
- Tom, Nick and Myrtle catch a train into New York. Myrtle does some shopping and buys a puppy. All three then go to an apartment which Tom and Myrtle use for their extra-marital affair. They are joined by Myrtle's sister Catherine, and by a couple named McKee. They drink whisky and talk until around midnight.
- Tom breaks Myrtle's nose, provoked by her repetition of Daisy's name. Nick leaves with McKee, who insists on showing him some of the photographs he has taken.
- At Pennsylvania Station, Nick waits to catch the 4 a.m. train home.

ANALYSIS

THE WEST AND THE WASTE LAND

The action of *The Great Gatsby* takes place on America's East coast. Nick Carraway is narrating this story after he has moved back home to the Midwest, physically the heart of America. Yet, in the final chapter, Nick says 'this has been a story of the West, after all' (p. 167). He means that it has been a story of the conflict between dreams and the harsh realities of the world, a tale of hope struggling against disillusionment.

For European settlers, arriving on the East coast, America had long been seen as a fresh New World. Moving West, across the continent, was a way to keep that dream alive. Until the last years of the nineteenth century, there were still some areas of land in the American West that hadn't been occupied and settled. But more importantly the West had become a rich symbol of hope, rebirth and unlimited potential to realise your dreams.

On the East coast, in 1922, wealthy New Yorkers drive around in flashy cars, but the unsuccessful garage mechanic George Wilson lives with his wife Myrtle in a dust covered 'valley of ashes' (p. 26). It is a dismal spot where waste from the city is dumped. They have lived there for eleven years, but now Myrtle has a dream. She longs to leave her past behind and to start a new life with Tom. But in reality Tom has no intention of leaving Daisy; he simply uses Myrtle as his mistress.

Note how Jay Gatsby's dream that Daisy will leave Tom resembles Myrtle's dream that Tom will leave Daisy. Note too that both Gatsby and Myrtle are violently killed – Myrtle by Tom's wife; Gatsby by Myrtle's husband. Are both dreams equally unrealistic? Are Gatsby and Myrtle really in love with Daisy and Tom, or are they simply obsessed with what the Buchanans represent?

The year 1922, in which *The Great Gatsby* is set, saw the publication of T. S. Eliot's *The Waste Land*. That poem registered Eliot's sense that spiritual values had been lost in the increasingly materialistic modern world. Fitzgerald's 'valley of ashes' (p. 26) is literally a waste land, but it can also be read figuratively as an image of a spiritually bleak world.

GRADE BOOSTER **A02**

Pay close attention to the locations where the action of *The Great Gatsby* takes place. Fitzgerald does not use geography and landscape simply as background. Think about how these physical settings may contribute to your understanding of the characters and your interpretation of the action.

CONTEXT **A04**

A National Prohibition Act was passed in the United States in 1919 and remained in force until 1933. It placed severe restrictions upon the manufacture and distribution of alcoholic drinks. There are strong suggestions in this novel that Gatsby's wealth is due, in part at least, to his involvement with the unlawful supply of alcohol, or 'bootlegging' as it was known.

THE GATSBY BRAND

Myrtle was dismayed when she found out that her husband George had borrowed the suit he wore at their wedding (see p. 37). When she first met Tom Buchanan, on a train, she was immediately impressed by his suit, shirt and shoes. Unable to keep her eyes off Tom, she pretended to be looking at an advertisement over his head.

Advertising and brand names were a prominent feature of American life in the 1920s. The huge advertising hoarding, featuring Doctor Eckleburg's bespectacled eyes, is a realistic detail from America's early consumer culture. A visual advertisement of this kind couldn't be missed, and it could be understood by newly arrived immigrants with little or no grasp of English language. The optician's hoarding becomes really significant at the end of the novel, when George Wilson – in his bewilderment – mistakes those huge eyes for the eyes of God. Consumerism and materialism have taken the place of spiritual values in the America that Fitzgerald depicts in this novel.

Gatsby's efforts to attract Daisy can be seen as a kind of self-advertisement. He has created an image in order to persuade Daisy that he is the person she needs. In effect he is promoting his own brand. His clothes are imported from Europe, and are intended to impress Daisy just as Tom's clothes impress Myrtle. Note that in Chapter 8, Daisy actually tells Gatsby that he reminds her of an advertisement (see p. 114).

STUDY FOCUS: THE IMAGE A04

In recent decades, pop music icons have skilfully used the media to shape their own image and keep themselves in the public view. Long before that, Hollywood film stars also cultivated their image in the press and magazines. Myrtle Wilson reads movie magazines, and follows the celebrity gossip of the day.

When *The Great Gatsby* was published films were still silent, yet Hollywood stars were already world famous. Many Hollywood actors have changed their original name and created a new image. Marilyn Monroe (1926–62), for example, grew up being Norma Jeane Baker.

Try thinking about Jay Gatsby's image in the context of the new celebrity culture of the 1920s, and in terms of what you know about celebrity culture today.

CHECK THE BOOK A04

Susan Strasser's *Satisfaction Guaranteed: The Making of the American Mass Market* (Smithsonian Institute, 2004) is a fascinating account of the development of advertising, a culture of shopping and promotion of brand names in America during the early decades of the twentieth century.

CLASS

The Wilsons live over the garage where George works. This shows they have lower social standing than Nick Carraway, who works in the city but lives in a suburb, at a distance from work. The very rich in this novel seem not to work at all, and can live where they choose. Fitzgerald is indicating that America, despite claims to democratic equality, is a society divided into a number of social classes based on wealth and property. He was attracted to the lavish lifestyle of the wealthy, yet he also had a keen sense of social injustice in twentieth-century America.

GLOSSARY

30 **John D. Rockefeller** (1839–1937) wealthy oil tycoon

31 **ladies swinging in the gardens of Versailles** a reference to the famous picture *The Swing* (1766) by Jean Honoré Fragonard

31 ***Simon Called Peter*** a bestselling novel by Robert Keable (1887–1927) that tells the story of a young clergyman whose experiences during the First World War result in loss of religious faith

Broadway a street in New York, renowned for theatre

CHAPTER 3

SUMMARY

- Nick describes Gatsby's lifestyle, his servants, lavish parties, motorboats and cars.
- At one of Gatsby's parties, Nick talks with Jordan Baker and two girls she met at an earlier party. They discuss rumours that Gatsby has killed a man, and that he was a German spy in the First World War.
- In Gatsby's library, Nick and Jordan meet a man wearing glasses that make his eyes look owl-like. The owl-eyed man has been 'drunk for about a week' (p. 47).
- Nick meets Gatsby for the first time. Gatsby claims to have seen Nick during their army service in the First World War. They share memories of 'wet, grey little villages in France' (p. 48).
- Gatsby speaks privately with Jordan Baker. She then tells Nick that Gatsby has disclosed 'the most amazing thing' (p. 53).
- Leaving the party, Nick witnesses 'a bizarre and tumultuous scene' surrounding a car that has crashed into a ditch (p. 54).
- Nick's comments on what he has written so far. He remembers a news report which claimed that Jordan Baker had cheated in a golf tournament. He concludes, 'She was incurably dishonest' (p. 58). Nonetheless he admits to feeling 'a sort of tender curiosity' towards her (p. 58).

ANALYSIS

CONSPICUOUS CONSUMPTION

In Chapter 1, Nick tells us that he drives 'an old Dodge' (p. 9), an ordinary American make of car. Gatsby's British Rolls-Royce and his yellow station-wagon, like his mansion, motorboats, clothes and extravagant parties, mark him out as a rich man. The American sociologist Thorstein Veblen (1857–1929), in his book *The Theory of the Leisure Class: A Study of Economic Institutions* (1899), used the term 'conspicuous consumption' to describe how the rich display their wealth through possessions. Gatsby's lifestyle is a blatant example of 'conspicuous consumption'.

Henry Ford (1863–1947), who pioneered car manufacture in the United States, promoted his cars as democratic vehicles, cheaply produced so that most Americans could afford to run one. Gatsby's expensive cars are part of his plan to impress Daisy; they are meant to stand out from the crowd. Eventually, they play a key role in Gatsby's downfall. Following Myrtle's death in Chapter 7, it is easy for George Wilson to track down the owner of the car that killed her.

THE OLD WORLD AND THE NEW WORLD

We are told that the invitation Gatsby sends to Nick is signed 'in a majestic hand' (p. 43). The notion of majesty, suggested by the adjective 'majestic', belongs to the old-fashioned and traditional social context of European monarchy, not to the dynamic modern world of democratic America. At his parties, Jay Gatsby watches events unfold with the dignity and detachment of an Old World monarch, but at heart he remains a passionate American boy.

In contrast to Gatsby's cool demeanour, his guests take advantage of every opportunity to have fun 'according to the rules of behaviour associated with an amusement park' (p. 43). Amusement parks were a popular feature of New York life in the 1920s.

Nick is struck by the number of young Englishmen present at the party, 'all well dressed, all looking a little hungry, and all talking in low, earnest voices to solid, prosperous Americans' (p. 43). These young Englishmen resemble characters in the work of Henry James (1843–1916), an American-born novelist who became a British subject in 1915. James wrote many stories and novels in which wealthy yet unsophisticated Americans come into contact with sophisticated yet impoverished Europeans.

The Great Gatsby frequently makes use of this distinction between the energetic and prosperous New World and the Old World, culturally rich yet damaged by war and tired from its long history. The book seems to ask whether America is doomed to repeat Europe's mistakes.

STUDY FOCUS: LIGHTS, CAMERA, ACTION **A02**

The Great Gatsby is a book about a man – Nick Carraway – writing a book about another man – Jay Gatsby – who has remained obsessively in love with a woman – Daisy Fay – whom he met when they were teenagers. Daisy is now married to Tom Buchanan, so a lot of this story is about Gatsby's hope that one day he and Daisy will be together again as lovers. In itself that does not amount to a dramatic, action-packed storyline. Look carefully at the way Fitzgerald creates and connects scenes that hold our attention, rather like a film director who cleverly keeps us watching.

The party in this chapter is part of Gatsby's attempt to impress Daisy. There is plenty of action on the surface: people coming and going, chance meetings, high spirits and drunken behaviour. In itself much of this action is going nowhere, in terms of the development of the story, but as we watch it unfold we are drawn deeper into the heart of Gatsby's obsession.

REVISION FOCUS: TASK 2 **A02**

How far do you agree with the statements below?

- Gatsby's wild parties reflect the turmoil in his heart as he yearns to be with Daisy.
- Fitzgerald portrays America as a land of broken promises and shattered dreams.

Try writing opening paragraphs for essays based on the discussion points above. Set out your arguments clearly.

GATSBY THE SHOWMAN

Owl Eyes is impressed by the lengths to which Gatsby has gone in creating his image. 'What thoroughness! What realism!' he says, when he discovers that there are actual books on the library shelves rather than just cardboard spines pretending to be books (p. 47). He notes though that the pages remain uncut; these are volumes that have been bought to create an impression rather than to read.

Owl Eyes compares Gatsby to David Belasco (1853–1931), a Broadway theatre producer renowned for the painstaking realism of his stage settings. Remember that Gatsby's mentor was Dan Cody, who shares his surname with Buffalo Bill Cody, the famous Wild West showman.

CRITICAL VIEWPOINT **A02**

The 'violent confusion' (p. 54) of the comic scene in which a car has crashed into a ditch after leaving the drive of Gatsby's mansion can be seen to **foreshadow** the accident that results in Myrtle Wilson's tragic death. Owl Eyes is here accused of being 'a bad driver' (p. 55), but he reveals that another man was actually driving. Later, Gatsby takes responsibility for Myrtle's death, even though Daisy was driving. Details in this **narrative** are intricately intertwined.

PART OF THE STORY

After describing one of Gatsby's parties at some length, Nick Carraway steps back to examine his telling of the story so far. In doing so, he reminds us of the fact that he is a writer as well as our **narrator**. Events which seem so immediate when we are caught up in the **dialogue** and description have actually been filtered through his remembering and reconstruction of them. Nick is part of the story in a fundamental way. We are learning about Nick as he tells us about Gatsby.

Think about the kind of character Nick says he is. Then look at the way he is writing this story. He presents himself as reserved and rather ordinary. But is that the kind of man you would expect to describe Gatsby's party in sentences such as, 'In his blue gardens men and girls came and went like moths among the whisperings and the champagne and the stars' (p. 41)?

'Most of the time I worked' (p. 56), Nick tells us. His job in New York's financial sector involves selling bonds and reading up on investments. During the day he is surrounded by other office workers, people he knows on first-name terms, who eat run-of-the-mill food in dingy restaurants. Nick enters another world, a world of dreams and imagination, when he meets Jay Gatsby, who hosts lavish parties and provides expensive food and drink for guests he scarcely knows.

Nick tells us he has had a brief affair with a girl, until her brother scared him off. Why should Nick provoke the brother's 'mean looks' (p. 57)? He presents himself as decent, unassuming and respectable and at the end of this chapter he declares, 'I am one of the few honest people that I have ever known' (p. 59). What could the girl's brother find objectionable in such a straightforward and restrained individual as Nick, who keeps his emotions under control and avoids the kind of intense feelings experienced by Jay Gatsby. The two men seem poles apart in temperament. But could it be that Gatsby embodies passion and desire that Nick himself feels, but won't acknowledge?

CHECK THE BOOK A03

Fitzgerald, the actual author of *The Great Gatsby*, has made Nick Carraway both a character who participates in the action and the storyteller, reflecting on events and writing it down. Fitzgerald was influenced by the example of the Polish-born British novelist Joseph Conrad (1857–1924) who used a comparable **narrative** device in his short novel *Heart of Darkness* (1902; Penguin Books, 2007).

STUDY FOCUS: NICK IN LOVE A02

Nick seems to give us a valuable insight into his emotional life when he refers to 'romantic women' (p. 57), whom he chases after, but only in his imagination. Love affairs seem to attract Nick as an idea, but in reality he seems to find it difficult to become fully involved with a woman. He seems to worry that people might find out about his love affairs and disapprove of them. Yet towards the end of the next chapter, Nick puts his arm around Jordan Baker's 'golden shoulder' (p. 77), draws her close to him and invites her to dinner. There seems to be inconsistency here. Is Nick being entirely honest with us? As well as his involvement with Jordan, he is still in touch with a girl in the Midwest. He tells us: 'I'd been writing letters once a week and signing them: "Love Nick,"' and he adds, 'there was a vague understanding that had to be tactfully broken off before I was free' (p. 59).

42 **Castile** a province in central Spain

Gilda Gray's understudy Gilda Gray (1901–59), who changed her name from Marianne Michalski, came from a Polish immigrant family, and sang in Midwestern bars before being discovered by the impresario Florenz Ziegfeld (1869–1932). She was the highly paid star of his 1922 *Follies* and was best known for her scandalously suggestive 'shimmy' dance

47 **Volume One of the *Stoddard Lectures*** John L. Stoddard (1850–1931), the author of numerous travel books, and father of Lothrop Stoddard, who wrote *The Rising Tide of Color Against White World-Supremacy*

Belasco David Belasco (1853–1931) was an American dramatist and theatre manager, founder of the Belasco Theater in New York, who gained notoriety for the extravagance of his production methods, in the service of greater realism on stage

KEY QUOTATIONS: CHAPTER 3 **A01**

Key quotation 1: 'I wasn't actually in love, but I felt a sort of tender curiosity' (p. 58).

Possible interpretations:

- Nick is aware of his feelings and controls his emotions.
- Nick has strong feelings for Jordan despite her cynicism and dishonesty.
- Nick feels uneasy with the feeling of being in love, yet he admires Gatsby for his intense devotion to Daisy.

Key quotation 2: 'I am one of the few honest people that I have ever known' (p. 59).

Possible interpretations:

- Nick recognises that most people he knows are dishonest.
- Nick values the truth in a world filled with illusion and deception.
- Or perhaps Nick is deluding himself when he denies his own dishonesty, or self-deception.

Other useful quotations:

- 'I believe that on the first night I went to Gatsby's house I was one of the few guests who had actually been invited. People were not invited – they went there' (p. 43)
- 'A high Gothic library, panelled with carved English Oak, and probably transported complete from some ruin overseas' (p. 46)
- Jordan says to Nick, 'It takes two to make an accident'. Then she adds, 'I hate careless people. That's why I like you.' (p. 59)
- Nick on his own character: 'I am slow-thinking and full of interior rules that act as brakes on my desires, and I knew that first I had to get myself definitely out of that tangle back home.' (p. 59)

GRADE BOOSTER **A04**

It is important to show that you know *The Great Gatsby* is not a straightforwardly realistic novel. Nick refers to specific places in New York, the names of streets and buildings, historical figures and events; all these details create a sense of reality. The action of this book is connected to places that can be found on maps. But throughout *The Great Gatsby* factual details are interwoven with the workings of imagination.

CONTEXT **A04**

Gatsby's library is decorated in Gothic style. This was the dominant architectural style in western Europe during the Middle Ages. Gothic became fashionable again in Victorian England, and a fusion of Gothic and modern design was popular in America between 1900 and 1930. A notable example of that ornate style is the Woolworth Building, in New York's Manhattan district. Built in 1913, it was known during the 1920s as the Cathedral of Commerce.

CHAPTER 4

SUMMARY

- Gatsby visits Nick for the first time. Nick notices Gatsby's restlessness 'continually breaking through his punctilious manner' (pp. 62–3).
- Gatsby tells Nick about his Midwestern upbringing, his war service, his promotion to the rank of major and his education at Oxford University. Nick senses that Gatsby is not telling the truth. Gatsby alludes to a sad thing that has happened to him.
- Gatsby introduces Nick to Meyer Wolfshiem. Later, Gatsby explains that Wolfshiem illegally fixed the outcome of the 1919 World Series baseball tournament.
- Nick introduces Gatsby to Tom Buchanan. Gatsby makes a sudden departure, clearly embarrassed.
- Jordan tells Nick about the occasion in 1917 when she saw Daisy with Jay Gatsby, then a young lieutenant. Gatsby had been sent to Europe, and was promoted to the rank of major. Meanwhile, Daisy had married Tom Buchanan.
- Jordan tells Nick that she found Daisy, on the day before her wedding, drunk and clutching a letter sent by Gatsby. Soon after the wedding, Daisy became pregnant, and Tom started to have affairs with other women.
- Jordan tells Nick that Gatsby has asked to be invited to his house at a time when Daisy is also present. Nick kisses Jordan.

ANALYSIS

WHAT'S IN A NAME?

The list of guests who visit Gatsby's party is a comic set piece. The tone is quite distinct from the lyrical style that Nick often uses. Note that there are plant names here – 'Hornbeam', 'Endive', 'Orchid', 'Duckweed'; animal names – 'Civet', 'Blackbuck', 'Beaver', 'Ferret', 'Klipspringer'; and names of sea creatures – 'Whitebait', 'Hammerhead', 'Beluga'.

Some of these names make the partygoers seem like caricatures rather than rounded and realistic characters. This should draw our attention to the impact a name can have. Remember that *The Great Gatsby* tells the story of a man who has changed his name, for a reason. James Gatz becomes Jay Gatsby so that he may appear to be a more glamorous individual.

The Great Gatsby shares its name with its central character. Paying attention to the names of characters can tell you a lot. Remember that the history of America has involved the arrival of immigrants from different parts of the world. You can see from his name that Tom Buchanan has Scottish ancestry, for example, and that Meyer Wolfshiem's family origins are Jewish. Gatz is a Germanic name, and remember that America had recently been at war with Germany. Gatsby is more difficult to pin down in terms of origin. It also has a more sophisticated sound than the monosyllabic Gatz.

Daisy's surname prior to marriage was Fay, which is a long-established Irish surname. 'Fay' is also an old English word for fairy. Daisy is a creature from an enchanted world, in Gatsby's eyes. Together with her flowery first name, the surname Fay suggests that she is delicate, and physically Daisy appears so. But as we learn more about her character that air of delicacy seems increasingly misleading.

CONTEXT **A04**

Nick wrote his list of visitors to Gatsby's house on a timetable, or schedule, dated 5 July 1922. That calendar detail tells us when the action of this novel took place. It is also the day after Independence Day, when Americans annually celebrate the break with Europe in 1776, which ties in with the book's New World theme.

STUDY FOCUS: WORDS AND MEANING `A02`

Fitzgerald makes his **narrator**, Nick Carraway, use language in unexpected and sometimes peculiar ways. This may be figurative (**metaphor** and **simile**), or poetic, or playful. Watch out for the effects achieved through his use of unusual vocabulary or symbolic language. Think carefully about how Nick's style of storytelling and his choice of words affect your understanding of the story itself and the characters. Is Nick's narrating style part of the novel's more general concern with issues of style and appearance? Can we make a comparison between Nick's words and Gatsby's shirts and suits? Are both designed to project an image, or to conceal something?

RACE AND ORGANISED CRIME

Organised crime had a big impact on life in American cities, such as New York and Chicago, during the 1920s. Prominent gangsters often came from non-Anglo-Saxon backgrounds. They were keen to succeed in America, but found lawful routes to success blocked to them, because of their origins. The famous gangster Al Capone was a son of Italian immigrants; Dean O'Bannion and his North Side Mob in Chicago were Irish Americans; 'Bugsy' Siegel and Meyer Lansky came from Eastern European Jewish families.

There are numerous strong suggestions in this novel that Jay Gatsby has links with such underworld figures. His involvement with Meyer Wolfshiem seems to confirm that he has criminal connections. Wolfshiem is a professional gambler, 'the man who fixed the World's Series back in 1919' (p. 71). Nick thinks of this as a betrayal by one man of the belief in fair play of fifty million baseball fans, an unethical act as well as a major crime performed by Wolfshiem 'with the single-mindedness of a burglar blowing a safe' (p. 71).

STARTING AFRESH

As Gatsby drives him from Long Island to Manhattan, crossing the East River, Nick observes: 'The city seen from the Queensboro Bridge is always the city seen for the first time, in its first wild promise of all the mystery and the beauty in the world' (p. 67). This reaction to New York **foreshadows** the passage in the final chapter where Nick imagines a Dutch sailor seeing for the first time 'the fresh green breast of the new world' (p. 171). America seemed to offer Europeans a chance to start afresh. Nick still feels the sense of a new beginning as he enters New York City. When Nick grasps the intense nature of Gatsby's love for Daisy, and realises that his neighbour has bought a mansion in order to live across the bay from her, he remarks, 'He came alive to me, delivered suddenly from the womb of his purposeless splendour' (p. 76). Nick has regarded him as a flashy character, but Gatsby is now reborn for him as a passionate man with deep feelings and a purpose in life.

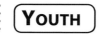

Note that in 1917, when Gatsby first met her, Daisy was just eighteen. Jordan was only sixteen at that time. So in 1922, when the action of the novel takes place, they are both still young. Jordan is just twenty-one, yet she is cynical and is said to be dishonest and a cheat. Despite these character flaws, Nick is clearly attracted to her.

Nick likes to present himself as a detached and rather cold person, who at thirty is too old for youthful excitement and strong feelings. Yet here he physically holds and kisses Jordan Baker. Gatsby, clinging to his memories of an adolescent love affair with Daisy, remains alone, living in hope. Nick, on the other hand, gets involved with Jordan in a way that may seem opportunistic, and certainly doesn't seem ideal.

America has cultivated an image as a youthful nation, full of energy and hope. Remember though that the New World settled by European immigrants had for centuries before their arrival been inhabited by Native Americans. The Europeans took the land, often by force. That fact, and the enslavement of Africans until the mid-nineteenth century, reveal a violent reality underlying America's youthful self-image.

REVISION FOCUS: TASK 3 · A02

How far do you agree with the statements below?

● Jordan Baker is a more honest character than Jay Gatsby.
● America is presented in this novel as a land of delusion and injustice.

Try writing opening paragraphs for essays based on the discussion points above. Set out your arguments clearly.

CHECK THE BOOK · A04

Howard Zinn's *A People's History of the United States* (Harper Perennial Modern Classics, 2010) is an acclaimed account of America's past that shows how the actual conditions of people's lives have often been at odds with the nation's ideals and aspirations.

GLOSSARY

60 **bootlegger** someone involved in the illegal production and distribution of alcoholic drink. Manufacture and supply of alcohol was prohibited in America during the 1920s

Von Hindenburg Paul von Hindenburg (1847–1934), soldier and second president of Germany

64 **the Argonne Forest** in 1918 American troops fought a battle against Germans in this region of north-east France, close to the border with Belgium

65 **little Montenegro** a small, mountainous kingdom in south-eastern Europe

'Orderi di Danilo' … Nicolas Rex a medal named after Prince Danilo I, who ruled Montenegro from 1852 until 1860. King Nicolas ruled the country between 1910 and 1918

66 **jug-jug-*spat*!** in his poem 'The Nightingale' (1798), Samuel Taylor Coleridge (1772–1834), following poetic convention, describes that bird's song as a 'musical and swift jug jug'. Fitzgerald is here deflating that conventional Romantic representation of a nightingale's song

67 **the Queensboro Bridge** this bridge spans New York City's East River, joining the districts of Queens and Manhattan

Blackwell's Island an island that lies beneath the Queensboro Bridge, in the East River

68 **The old Metropole** a hotel in Manhattan

Rosy Rosenthal Herman Rosenthal testified against police corruption in New York. He was murdered in June 1912 by a gang which included a police officer, Charlie Becker. The murderers were executed in 1915

73 **Camp Taylor** in 1918 Fitzgerald, serving in the American army, was stationed at Camp Zachary Taylor, near Louisville, Kentucky

75 **Santa Barbara** a fashionable resort on the coast of California, north of Los Angeles

76 **I'm the Sheik of Araby** a popular song of the time

KEY QUOTATIONS: CHAPTER 4   A01

Key quotation 1: Of Meyer Wolfshiem, Gatsby says: 'He's the man who fixed the World's Series back in 1919' (p. 71).

Possible interpretations:

- Introduces a real historical incident into the fictional narrative.
- Suggests that Gatsby has criminal connections.
- Shows how even American sport has been corrupted in the pursuit of wealth.

Key quotation 2: 'He came alive to me, delivered suddenly from the womb of his purposeless splendour' (p. 76)

Possible interpretations:

- The moment when Nick starts to see Gatsby as a romantic hero, driven by his love for Daisy.
- Connects with other images of birth and new beginnings.
- Contrasts with the apparently purposeless lives led by other wealthy characters in the novel.

Other useful quotations:

- Gatsby's restlessness: 'continually breaking through his punctilious manner' (p. 63)
- Nick of Gatsby: 'I wondered whether there wasn't something a little sinister about him, after all' (p. 64)
- Gatsby: 'I lived like a young rajah in all the capitals of Europe' (p. 64)
- Wolfshiem says, 'Gatsby's very careful about women. He would never so much as look at a friend's wife.' (p. 70)
- Jordan, of Gatsby, 'You see, he's regular tough underneath it all' (p. 77).

GRADE BOOSTER   A02

When you comment on events or characters in this novel, bear in mind that Nick is presenting them to us. Pay attention not only to what he writes about, but also to the way he writes. Look at his style and vocabulary. What kind of a storyteller is Nick Carraway? Always remember, however, that F. Scott Fitzgerald is behind the scenes, creating Nick, along with the other characters.

CHAPTER 5

SUMMARY

- When Nick gets home, at two o'clock the next morning, he finds that Gatsby's house is brightly lit.
- Gatsby – still awake – talks with him, discussing his plan to meet Daisy at Nick's house.
- On the day arranged for Gatsby's meeting with Daisy, it rains heavily. While Gatsby and Daisy talk, Nick wanders into his garden and looks at the neighbouring mansion, Gatsby's home.
- When Nick returns to the room he notices that Daisy has been crying.
- Nick and Daisy go with Gatsby to look at his house. It is filled with items imported from Europe, including clothes sent from England. Daisy is overwhelmed by Gatsby's 'beautiful shirts' (p. 89).
- Nick is struck by the intensity of the relationship between Gatsby and Daisy. After a while, he leaves them alone together.

ANALYSIS

IN THE LIGHT

Nick describes Gatsby, glowing after his conversation with Daisy, as 'an ecstatic patron of recurrent light' (p. 86). This is poetic language, rich with potential meaning. It makes Gatsby seem an extraordinary figure, with an almost god-like capacity to dispense light or restore sunshine after the rain. Earlier, on a more mundane level, we have witnessed Gatsby's extravagant use of electric lighting in his house and at his parties.

Nick compares Gatsby's mansion, ablaze with light, with the World's Fair (see p. 79). Fitzgerald was probably referring specifically to the International Exposition of Science, Arts and Industries held in the Bronx area of New York City in 1918. This combined an amusement park with exhibitions showing the latest scientific and technological innovations. Such events are designed not only to educate and entertain the public, but also to promote the image of the host nation.

We might choose to read the blazing lights of Gatsby's house as an image of his blazing love for Daisy. Or we may see it as a form of display, using electricity as he uses his cars and clothes in the hope of attracting Daisy's attention and drawing her to him. Note that, later in this chapter, in sunshine following a spell of rain, Gatsby remarks to Nick: 'My house looks well, doesn't it?' and he adds 'See how the whole front of it catches the light?' (p. 87).

EUROPE AND AMERICA

Gatsby's mansion has a 'feudal silhouette' (p. 88), like a building from the feudal society of the European Middle Ages. But ironically that silhouette is cast by modern electric lighting. The mansion was built by a brewer who wanted to live like an Old World lord of the manor, with his loyal workers housed in old-fashioned straw-thatched cottages. But note that the American workers refused to accept the straw roofs; they are not Old World peasants.

In medieval feudal life, the relationship between the ruling class and the peasantry was unchanging. People accepted their place in society. In a modern democracy with a capitalist

---

CONTEXT A04

In 1878, from his laboratory in Menlo Park, New Jersey, Thomas Alva Edison (1847–1931), inventor of the incandescent light bulb, announced to a world then lit by gas that it was possible to install domestic electric lighting. This was the same year that he invented the phonograph and opened up the world of sound recording. Known popularly as 'the wizard of Menlo Park', Edison also made major contributions to development of the telephone and the motion picture camera.

CRITICAL VIEWPOINT A02

Gatsby suggests to Nick that they should go to Coney Island, a New York resort famous for its brilliantly lit amusement parks (p. 79). Is Gatsby letting his cool image slip at this moment, descending to the level of his guests? Note how such small details in the **narrative** are patterned in ways that shed light on the way characters behave.

economy, the opposite is the case. Individuals are socially mobile. The brewer presumably lost his fortune when Prohibition prevented the manufacture of alcohol. Ironically, Jay Gatsby, who is allegedly a bootlegger, distributing alcohol illegally, has taken the brewer's place in the feudal mansion.

Gatsby tells Nick that he made enough money to buy this mansion in just three years. That expenditure would have been far beyond the income of most workers in 1920s America. Nick observes, 'Americans, while willing, even eager, to be serfs, have always been obstinate about being peasantry' (p. 86). Nick seems be suggesting that while Americans are prepared to do routine work – as George Wilson does – they will not accept the role of peasants, with no hope of changing and improving the condition of their own lives.

A self-made man, like Gatsby, would have been unthinkable in a feudal society, where everyone accepted their place in the social hierarchy. Nonetheless he seems to have made his money illegally, and importations from the Old World play a large part in his display of wealth. It's a complicated picture, with the Old World still clearly exerting an influence on New World thinking.

STUDY FOCUS: *THE GREAT* GATSBY?   A02

It seems that Fitzgerald was not entirely happy with the title *The Great Gatsby*. It creates certain expectations, making us eager to find out what makes Gatsby special. He stands out because of his wealth. But there are strong hints that he is rich because he is a criminal. Also, he is driven by his desire to steal away another man's wife. Ask yourself in what ways Jay Gatsby deserves to be called 'Great'. Pay careful attention to the way Fitzgerald handles the reunion between Daisy and Gatsby, a difficult scene to manage. Throughout the novel you should look out for ways in which the author is guiding the way we respond to Jay Gatsby.

REVISION FOCUS: TASK 4   A02

How far do you agree with the statements below?

- Daisy is not worthy of Gatsby's love.
- Jay Gatsby is not worthy of the epithet 'Great'.

Try writing opening paragraphs for essays based on the discussion points above. Set out your arguments clearly.

GRADE BOOSTER   A02

Many novels aim to present realistic action and characters. Think carefully about how writers create a sense of realism, piling up descriptive details, dates, names and other references that make you feel you are in a solid and familiar world. *The Great Gatsby* presents a familiar world up to a point, but Fitzgerald gives us the workings of Nick Carraway's memory and imagination rather than straightforward, uncomplicated facts.

GLOSSARY

83	**the secret of Castle Rackrent** *Castle Rackrent* is a novel, published in 1800 by the Anglo-Irish novelist Maria Edgeworth (1767–1849). It shows the downfall, due to extravagant living, of a family of Irish landowners	
85	**like Kant at his church steeple** Immanuel Kant (1724–1804) was a German philosopher who found that staring at a steeple in his home town, Königsberg, helped him to order his thoughts	
88	**the Merton College Library** Gatsby's library is modelled on this famous one at Oxford University	
	an Adam's study in the style of Robert Adam (1728–92), the neoclassical British architect	
90	**Mr Dan Cody** the surname evokes William Frederick 'Buffalo Bill' Cody (1846–1917), a Frontier scout who became a showman, organising popular Wild West shows which glamorised the pioneer lifestyle, and made him a lot of money in the process	
92	**'The Love Nest'** a popular song of 1920	

EXTENDED COMMENTARY

CHAPTER 5, PP. 88–9

The episode in which Gatsby and Daisy, reunited for a few hours after five years apart, visit his mansion carries an enormous amount of weight in the novel. Fitzgerald has already indicated to us that the real Daisy falls far short of the idealised Daisy who exists in Gatsby's heart and imagination. Now the author has to ensure that the encounter between these two characters is convincing.

Gatsby and Daisy have a lot of catching up to do. We might expect to hear them talk at length. Fitzgerald was a skilful writer of **dialogue**, but he keeps their conversation to a minimum. Their feelings are communicated through the way they act in this emotionally charged situation. We need to read their body language, to interpret their physical movements, which are notably awkward at first, and to be aware of what remains unsaid.

Daisy has never attended any of Gatsby's parties, so his mansion has the attraction of a new experience, the magic of a first encounter. Nick, on the other hand, feels the strangeness of being at the house without other guests. The relationship between the present and the past is thematically important to the novel as a whole, and it is particularly significant in this chapter, where we might expect the reunion of Gatsby and Daisy to be saturated with memories of their brief but intense love affair, five years earlier.

The description of Gatsby's mansion is highly economical yet it conveys his immense wealth and his painstaking stage management, with everything arranged in order to impress Daisy. Just before this passage, Daisy, with her floral name, has admired Gatsby's garden. Note that he has even taken pains over the scent of flowers growing there, 'the sparkling odour of jonquils and the frothy odour of hawthorn and plum blossoms and the pale gold odour of kiss-me-at-the-gate' (p. 88). The adjectives 'sparkling', 'frothy' and 'pale gold' suggest the fizz and colour of a glass of champagne.

In this passage Gatsby shows Daisy and Nick the upstairs rooms in his mansion. Here there are 'period bedrooms swathed in rose and lavender silk' (p. 88), imitating the luxury of an earlier historical period. Already, downstairs, we have encountered music-rooms in the style of Marie Antoinette. It also has Restoration Salons; rooms in the style of the age of Charles II.

In Gatsby's own apartment we discover he has not only a bedroom and a bath, but also a study. Owl Eyes told us in Chapter 3 that the pages of books in Gatsby's library remain uncut; despite a brief spell at Oxford University in reward for his war service, Gatsby is clearly not a studious man. But a study fits the sophisticated, aristocratic image this young man from the Midwest has tried to cultivate. The room is said to be in the elegant eighteenth-century architectural style of the Scottish brothers Robert Adam (1728–92) and James Adam (1730–94).

CONTEXT **A04**

Marie Antoinette was a French queen who was executed by revolutionaries in 1793. Charles II (1630–85) was restored to the English throne in 1660. His father, Charles I (1600–49), had been executed during the English Civil War by revolutionary forces under the leadership of Oliver Cromwell (1599–1658).

CONTEXT **A04**

America came into existence following the revolutionary overthrow of British rule in 1776. The American republic was founded on democratic ideals designed to set it apart from its European past. It is ironic that signs of success and status in the 1920s involve 'period bedrooms' and other imitations of the style of European monarchies.

The Adam brothers were historical figures, but words in *The Great Gatsby* often trigger associations in ways that enrich meaning. The surname Adam, might trigger an association with Adam in the Bible. Jay Gatsby, beginning his life afresh, might in some respects remind us of Adam, the first man created by God in a brand new world. Daisy might then be viewed in **archetypal** terms as Eve, tempting Adam to lose his innocence, with tragic consequences. The artificial, stage-managed world that Gatsby inhabits is, however, no Garden of Eden.

Gatsby, Nick and Daisy drink Chartreuse, a bright green liqueur. Note how this small detail, like many others, resonates with major themes of the novel. Its greenness fits into the novel's careful patterning of colours. It may remind us of the green light that burns all night at the end of Tom and Daisy's boat dock, and it anticipates the powerful image in the final chapter of a Dutch sailor encountering for the first time 'a fresh, green breast of the new world' (p. 171). Green suggests natural life and growth, and also a kind of innocence. In Gatsby's carefully cultivated world, however, grass is trimmed, flowers are cut and herbs flavour an alcoholic drink. Significantly, in America 'green' is slang for money, as it has historically been the colour of the dollar banknote.

CONTEXT A04

Chartreuse is an alcoholic drink containing herbs that has been made at a monastery near Grenoble, France since the 1740s. It is thus yet another importation from Europe, and another instance of alcohol being consumed during the time of Prohibition.

Gatsby is overwhelmed with emotion during Daisy's visit. When she uses his gold brush to smooth her hair, he watches, spellbound, trying to speak but unable to find the words to express his feelings. Nick observes that Gatsby 'was consumed with wonder at her presence' (p. 89). Note that the Dutch sailor, encountering 'a fresh, green breast of the new world' in the final chapter is said to have been a human being 'face to face for the last time in history with something commensurate to his capacity for wonder' (p. 171).

Is Fitzgerald suggesting that the awesome vision of America as a New World, with apparently limitless potential, has narrowed down to a point where wonder is no more than what Gatsby feels as he watches Daisy brush her hair in his bedroom? Or is that capacity for wonder perhaps the source of Gatsby's 'greatness'? Is it his sense of wonder that drives him to refuse to live the aimless and unsuccessful kind of life led by his parents?

CRITICAL VIEWPOINT A03

In Chapter 3, talking with Nick in Gatsby's library, Owl Eyes compares Gatsby to the theatrical director David Belasco (1853–1931), renowned for the painstaking realism of his stagecraft (p. 47). The mansion therefore appears not so much a home as an extravagant prop for Gatsby to display his wealth and declare his love for Daisy.

When the intensity of Gatsby's feelings leaves him unable to speak coherently, his props come the rescue. He opens two large cabinets that contain his clothes, declaring that he employs a man in England to buy them for him. Expensive linen, silk and flannel shirts are thrown in front of Daisy and Nick as symbols of Gatsby's success and sophistication. They take the place of words as a means to communicate with the woman he loves. As we know, in our own fashion-conscious times, the clothes you wear make a statement about the person you are, or think you are. But is it always the statement we intend to make? Others might read it differently. We might interpret the 'many coloured disarray' (p. 89) of Gatsby's shirts as nothing more than a disclosure of the turmoil of his inner life.

In response Daisy cries 'stormily' (p. 89). Note the turbulence implied by that adjective. Why should a collection of fashion items create a storm within Daisy? She offers an explanation: 'It makes me sad because I've never seen such – such beautiful shirts before' (p. 89). As readers we are left to conclude that while our attention is directed to these beautiful shirts, the hearts of two former lovers are beating in deep disarray.

CHAPTER 6

SUMMARY

- Nick tells us that an inquisitive newspaper reporter visited Gatsby one morning; rumours about him had spread to a point where 'he fell just short of being news' (p. 94).
- Nick then tells us what he knows of Gatsby's real life-story. His original name was James Gatz and he grew up in North Dakota.
- At seventeen James Gatz changed his name to the more glamorous Jay Gatsby.
- He met Dan Cody, who had become wealthy prospecting for precious metals. Cody became Gatsby's mentor, teaching him how to get rich.
- Nick tells us about an occasion when Tom Buchanan visits Gatsby's mansion. Gatsby tells Tom that he knows Daisy.
- Tom and Daisy Buchanan attend a party at Gatsby's mansion.
- Gatsby and Daisy spend half an hour together, sitting on the steps of Nick's house.
- Tom suggests to Nick that Gatsby is a criminal bootlegger, like a lot of newly rich Americans at that time.
- Gatsby is upset that Daisy has not enjoyed the party. He wants her to leave her husband and marry him.

ANALYSIS

BEING AND BECOMING

In his first novel, *This Side of Paradise* (1920), Fitzgerald writes of his main character, a young man named Amory Blaine: 'It was always the becoming he dreamed of, never the being.' In *The Great Gatsby*, we are told that Jay Gatsby's parents lived in one place, and worked within the fixed pattern of a farming life. His parents were solidly 'being' themselves. Gatsby, on the other hand, dreams, like Amory Blaine, of 'becoming' someone. He does not want his identity to be pinned down.

Nick tells us that Gatsby was the son of 'shiftless and unsuccessful farm people' (p. 95). His parents lived off the land, but to him their lives seemed aimless. At seventeen, Gatsby met Dan Cody, who lived on a yacht and was a millionaire. As farmers, his parents had a fixed place to live and work; Cody, on the other hand, was mobile and energetic and that attracted Gatsby. He left his parents behind – 'his imagination had never really accepted them as his parents at all' (p. 95) – and went off with Cody, who showed him another way of living a life.

Nick tells us that, when he met him, there was a persistent rumour that Gatsby 'didn't live in a house at all, but in a boat that looked like a house and was moved secretly up and down the Long Island shore' (p. 94). This rumour, though untrue, should remind us of Gatsby's earlier life on Cody's yacht, which had represented for him 'all the beauty and glamour in the world' (p. 96). It should also remind us of Gatsby's determination not to be fixed in place and identity like his parents.

When Europeans started to arrive in America and decided to establish farming communities, they were often referred to as 'settlers'. America's past is a history of settlement. But it is also a history of restless movement.

CONTEXT A04

During the last quarter of the nineteenth century, the discovery of easily collected mineral ores caused prospectors to rush to make their fortune. The Yukon Territory, in the far North, saw a rush for gold. Nevada, in the West, saw a rush for silver. In both cases, the dream was to get rich quickly. A few, like Dan Cody in this novel, succeeded, but the reality was often disappointment and hardship.

IDEALISM AND MATERIALISM

Nick tells us, 'The truth was that Jay Gatsby of West Egg, Long Island, sprang from his Platonic conception of himself' (p. 95). Plato was an ancient Greek philosopher who argued that there is an ideal world beyond the material world in which we live. Our human senses are too crude to grasp this ideal world. The suggestion here is that seventeen-year-old Jay Gatsby, unhappy with his material circumstances, has created a ideal version of himself. His dreams and vivid imaginings have convinced him of 'the unreality of reality' (p. 95). His ideal has become more real to him than the physical world around him.

Gatsby was introduced to a wealthy lifestyle by the highly materialistic Dan Cody, and has developed his own image on the basis of material success achieved through illegal activity. Cody became a millionaire, but Nick tells us that under the surface he remained 'the pioneer debauchee, who during one phase of American life brought back to the Eastern seaboard the savage violence of the frontier brothel and saloon' (p. 97). A pioneer might seem heroic, but Fitzgerald reminds us that actual life at the Frontier was often violent and dangerous.

STUDY FOCUS: ACCIDENTS WILL HAPPEN — A02

In this chapter, James Gatz seems to seize control of his own destiny when he changes his name and starts to create a new life as Jay Gatsby. But it was his chance meeting with Dan Cody that really made the difference, and in Chapter 8, Gatsby acknowledges that it was a 'colossal accident' (p. 141) that led him to Daisy Fay's house.

In Chapter 1, Daisy asks Nick, 'What do people plan?' (p. 17). Jay Gatsby tries to plan the course of his life; he tries to design events in order to win Daisy's love. But his plans end in disaster. Accidents occur frequently in this novel – car crashes, in particular. Pay close attention to the plans made by characters in *The Great Gatsby*, and to the role of accidents in the **narrative**.

REVISION FOCUS: TASK 5 — A02

How far do you agree with the statements below?

- Crime is made to seem glamorous in this novel.
- Nick often uses language in a way that is too self-consciously literary.

Try writing opening paragraphs for essays based on the discussion points above. Set out your arguments clearly.

A KIND OF MAGIC

As Daisy sings, Nick hears in her husky voice 'a little of her warm human magic' (p. 104). Nick then imagines the arrival of some radiant young woman who might make Gatsby forget his years of devotion to Daisy, in 'one moment of magical encounter' (p. 105). The term 'magic' is here used to refer to that strange quality of attraction often described as a form of enchantment, or associated with falling under a spell.

CONTEXT — A04

In *The Republic*, his blueprint for a model society, the Greek philosopher Plato (*c.*427–347 BC) argues that the material world is illusory; our physical senses are too crude to grasp the true nature of reality, which exists in ideal forms. In Plato's republic divisions of social class are rigid. It is impossible for members of the warrior or working classes to adopt the lifestyle of the aristocracy, whose souls are superior.

CONTEXT — A04

The best-known stage magician amongst Fitzgerald's contemporaries was Harry Houdini (1874–1926), an immigrant from Hungary who changed his name from Ehrich Weiss. As a young man, Houdini performed at Coney Island amusement park, but later he achieved worldwide fame and featured in several silent films.

A more down-to-earth kind of magic might be suggested by the name 'The Great Gatsby'. It is the kind of name often adopted by stage magicians and illusionists. Is Gatsby, after all, no more than a showman, dealing in illusions? Or can we detect another kind of magic in the way that he transforms himself from an ordinary Midwestern boy into a glamorous man of mystery? Or when he transforms Daisy Fay, within his own imagination, from a pretty Louisville girl to an ideal of radiant life and beauty?

TIME PASSES

Nick warns, 'You can't repeat the past'. Gatsby replies, 'Why of course you can!' (p. 106). This is an illustration of Gatsby's 'extraordinary gift for hope' (p. 8), but we can see that he is deluded. The future he imagines for himself is actually focused in a moment that is forever lost in the past, the magical moment when he fell in love with Daisy Fay.

Remember that Gatsby has tried to delete much of his past; to erase all traces of his family and his upbringing in the Midwest. But the last words of the final chapter of *The Great Gatsby* confirm that we can never escape the flow of time: 'So we beat on, boats against the current, borne back ceaselessly into the past' (p. 172). That sentence is carved into Fitzgerald's gravestone.

STUDY FOCUS: MEMORIES AND DREAMS A02

In Chapter 5, Gatsby, who is emotionally drained by his reunion with Daisy, is said to be 'running down like an over-wound clock' (p. 89). In Chapter 6, an old clock ticks on young Jay Gatsby's washstand (p. 95). This clock measures the passing of the hours mechanically, but Gatsby experiences time in a very different way, through his memories of the past and in dreams of the future.

A SENSE OF WONDER

His love for Daisy, makes Gatsby feel that he can 'suck on the pap of life, gulp down the incomparable milk of wonder' (p. 107). The image is of a child at its mother's breast, being nourished with the 'milk of wonder'. 'Wonder' is a key word in this novel.

This image of 'the pap of life' **foreshadows** the reference at the end of *The Great Gatsby* to 'a fresh, green breast of the new world', a vision that can match the human 'capacity for wonder' (p. 171).

Note that between these moments of wonder, however, Myrtle Wilson is hit by a car, and we are told that 'her left breast was swinging loose like a flap' (p. 131). This is a shocking image of a literal rather than a figurative breast. *The Great Gatsby* is a novel in which the material world is repeatedly shown to be in conflict with visionary ideals.

CHECK THE BOOK A04

James Gatz is said to 'invent' Jay Gatsby. Fitzgerald's English contemporary D. H. Lawrence (1885–1930), in his *Studies in Classic American Literature* (1923), identifies 'plumbing' and 'saving the World' as 'the two great American specialities'. Lawrence makes a connection between the practical and the visionary aspects of American culture by suggesting that the invention of labour-saving machines has given Americans more free time for dreaming.

GLOSSARY		
94	**'underground pipe-line to Canada'**	it was rumoured during the Prohibition period that a hidden pipe-line existed to transport alcohol from Canada into the United States
95	*Tuolomee*	the yacht is named after a gold-mining area in the Sierra Nevada mountains of northern California
	Platonic conception	Plato (*c.*427–347 BC), a Greek philosopher
96	**Madame de Maintenon**	(1635–1719) the influential second wife of the French king Louis XIV

KEY QUOTATIONS: CHAPTER 6 A01

Key quotation 1: 'His parents were shiftless and unsuccessful farm people – his imagination had never really accepted them as his parents at all' (p. 95).

Possible interpretations:

- Even before he met Daisy, James Gatz desired more than the world he knew could offer him.
- Imagination is at the heart of Gatsby's character.
- Gatsby has to erase his past in order to become successful.

Key quotation 2: 'So he invented just the sort of Jay Gatsby that a seventeen-year-old boy would be likely to invent, and to this conception he was faithful to the end' (p. 95).

Possible interpretations:

- Gatsby is to be admired for his loyalty to a vision.
- Gatsby is to be pitied because he never grew up.
- The real Daisy is less important to Gatsby than an ideal version that matches his own ideal self.

Other useful quotations:

- Gatsby: 'his heart was in a constant, turbulent riot.' (p. 95)
- Gatsby: 'For a while these reveries provided an outlet for his imagination; they were a . . . promise that the rock of the world was founded securely on a fairy's wing.' (pp. 95–6)
- Tom: 'I may be old-fashioned in my ideas, but women run around too much these days to suit me' (p. 100)
- Gatsby: 'He knew that when he kissed this girl, and forever wed his unutterable visions to her perishable breath, his mind would never romp again like the mind of God' (p. 107)

GRADE BOOSTER A02

Think carefully about the relationship between fact and fiction in this novel. What are the facts? What do we actually know for sure? Gatsby has changed his identity and is surrounded by gossip and rumour. Nick is our guide to the events and characters in this story, but how far can we trust him? It is important to show that you recognise that the truth is not straightforward in *The Great Gatsby*.

CHECK THE BOOK A03

In classic American novels such as Mark Twain's *The Adventures of Huckleberry Finn* (1884) and Jack Kerouac's *On the Road* (1957) you find characters who are unable to settle, and feel the need to keep moving on. You find comparable characters in the American 'road movie', a cinematic genre that is as much about a restless state of mind as it is about motor cars.

CHAPTER 7

SUMMARY

- Daisy has been visiting Gatsby regularly. He has dismissed his servants to prevent the spread of gossip.
- On the hottest day of the summer, Nick and Gatsby have lunch with the Buchanans. They meet Daisy's daughter, Pammy. Tom recognises that Daisy and Gatsby are in love.
- They drive into New York: Tom takes Nick and Jordan; Gatsby travels with Daisy.
- Tom stops for petrol at George Wilson's garage, and is startled to learn that the Wilsons plan to go West.
- Tom, Daisy, Jordan, Nick and Gatsby take a room in the Plaza Hotel. Gatsby asserts that he is the only man Daisy has ever really loved. Tom scornfully alludes to Gatsby's links with the criminal underworld.
- The **narrative** cuts to an inquest where Michaelis, the Wilsons' neighbour, is a witness.
- Myrtle Wilson has been killed by a hit-and-run driver. A bystander testifies that the 'death car' was a big yellow vehicle (p. 131).
- In the garden of the Buchanans' home, Gatsby tells Nick that Daisy was driving the vehicle, and discloses that he intends to take the blame for Myrtle's death.

CONTEXT · A04

Horace Greeley (1811–72), editor of the *New York Tribune*, famously offered the advice 'Go West!' to Americans seeking opportunities for self-advancement. The phrase became a popular slogan, but westward movement was already firmly associated with the American dream of a fresh start or a new beginning.

ANALYSIS

STUDY FOCUS: FEELING THE HEAT · A02

A less skilful writer may have merely mentioned that the action in this chapter took place on the hottest day of the year. Fitzgerald uses the intense heat of the day to enrich the meaning of the story. The heat drains energy from the characters, yet the restless Buchanans still drive into the city. The wedding party at the Plaza hotel prompts the Buchanans to reminisce about another very hot day on which they were married. The heat makes people irritable and uncomfortable, and brings problems and disagreements to the surface. It intensifies the tensions that are developing in the novel. Just as location is important in this novel, so too is the weather in this chapter. Pay close attention to the ways in which Fitzgerald makes the heat seem totally natural, while using it to heighten dramatic elements in the narrative.

GO WEST

George Wilson tells Tom that he has lived at the garage too long and needs to move away. He plans to go West, taking Myrtle with him. The Wilsons have been in the 'valley of ashes' for eleven years. They have become fixed in that place, just as Gatsby's unsuccessful parents were stuck on their farm. Gatsby managed to moved away while still young, but George Wilson is older, poor and tired. His dream of a fresh start will not be realised.

Note that George Wilson's face looks 'green' in the sunlight (p. 117). Elsewhere in this novel the colour green is associated with natural freshness and growth, but in Wilson's case it suggests that he is unwell or that he is green with envy of Tom's wealth and power. Nick tells us that Wilson has been made ill by the shock of discovering that Myrtle has 'some sort of life apart from him in another world' (p. 118). He adds that Tom, for all his wealth and power, 'had made a parallel discovery less than an hour before' (p. 118) – that is, he had found out that Daisy has been seeing Gatsby.

A SENSE OF PURPOSE

In Chapter 4, Nick says that when he found out that Gatsby was driven by his intense love for Daisy, 'He came alive to me, delivered suddenly from the womb of his purposeless splendour' (p. 76). Gatsby has a sense of purpose which seems to be lacking in the lives of most of the characters in this novel. We might question whether his pursuit of Daisy is worthwhile; but in a world of drifters he does at least have a sense of direction in his life.

In the energy-sapping heat of Chapter 7, Daisy herself expresses a sense of purposeless drifting: 'What'll we do with ourselves this afternoon?' cried Daisy, 'and the day after that, and the next thirty years?' (p. 113). The very wealthy Buchanans have all they need and are able to move from place to place, but they have no goals or dreams. So Daisy wonders how they will spend the rest of their lives.

Remember that these characters are still quite young. But Nick Carraway grows melancholy as he realises that this day is his thirtieth birthday: 'Thirty – the promise of a decade of loneliness, a thinning list of single men to know, a thinning brief-case of enthusiasm, thinning hair' (p. 129). Nick's dismal vision of life's diminishing potential contrasts markedly with his earlier statement of appreciation for Gatsby's 'heightened sensitivity to the promises of life' (p. 8).

Two-thirds of the way through this long chapter, Nick returns home to Long Island, with Tom, Jordan, Daisy and Gatsby. At this point he writes, 'So we drove on toward death through the cooling twilight' (p. 129). We may think he is referring to the inevitable passage of time, and that he is gloomily envisaging the end of life that awaits them all. The sentence fits in well with his melancholy musings on being thirty, and getting older every day. But after a brief pause in the text, like a skilful cut from one scene to another in a film, Nick refers to an inquest, and we discover that Myrtle Wilson had been killed. They were, in fact, driving towards the scene of her death.

VIOLENCE

There is a lot of glamour and party-going in *The Great Gatsby*, but there is also a lot of violence. Myrtle Wilson, a woman who is said to have 'tremendous vitality' (p. 131), has had her nose broken by Tom Buchanan, and now she is killed by a car driven by Daisy. Remember that earlier that day Myrtle had seen Tom driving the 'death car' (p. 131); she later ran into the road, desperate to speak with him. This is not a straightforward accident, but a terrible and unforeseen outcome of her affair with Tom.

Descriptions of violent action can seem melodramatic, or just repulsive. Note the skill with which Fitzgerald presents Myrtle's death indirectly, through the testimony of Michaelis and other bystanders. Nick was not present at the incident, of course. But, reporting what others saw, he still manages to convey the horrific impact of Myrtle's mutilated body: 'her left breast was swinging loose like a flap, and there was no need to listen for the heart beneath' (p. 131).

The Great Gatsby is a highly patterned literary work, interweaving key themes, significant words and recurrent images. This description of Myrtle's severed breast may remind us of 'the pap of life' from which, in Chapter 6, Gatsby is said to 'gulp down the incomparable milk of wonder' (p. 107). It also foreshadows the reference, in Chapter 9, to 'a fresh, green breast of the new world' (p. 171). Those are visionary images, but Myrtle's torn breast is physically real, and her heart is no longer beating.

CHECK THE FILM `A03`

In the film *The Curious Case of Benjamin Button* (2008), loosely based upon a story by Fitzgerald, Brad Pitt plays a man who is born elderly and gets younger in appearance as time passes. Fitzgerald felt that life has a radiance when we are young that it loses as we grow older.

CONTEXT `A04`

An air of ruthless criminal violence surrounds Meyer Wolfshiem. Organised crime led to numerous killings on the streets of New York and Chicago during the 1920s. Remember too that both Nick and Gatsby were involved, just a few years earlier, in the First World War, a conflict in which millions of soldiers died, including more than 100,000 Americans.

SOCIAL MOBILITY

Tom accuses Gatsby of being 'Mr Nobody from Nowhere' (p. 123). America has for a long time taken pride in being a place where there is social mobility, a land where people can

make a fresh start and find success no matter what their background. But Tom Buchanan is saying that Gatsby is a social upstart and not to be trusted, because he doesn't have a well-established family background like his own.

Gatsby is a self-made man. Not just in terms of money – he has also made a whole new identity for himself. Tom, on the other hand, has inherited wealth and a lifestyle that recalls the Old World aristocracy. He has polo ponies and boasts of being 'the first man who ever made a stable out of a garage' (p. 113). Tom takes advantage of the conveniences that come with modern life, such as cars and telephones, but he wants to preserve a world of privilege. In converting a garage to a stable, he seems to be reversing the trend of history in which motor cars have irreversibly superseded horses when it comes to transport. But Tom's ponies are just for show, and remember that George Wilson, a poor working man, depends on his own garage for survival.

CLASS DISTINCTIONS

At the start of his narration, Nick mentions a Carraway family tradition that 'we're descended from the Dukes of Buccleuch' (p. 8), although in fact the Carraways run a hardware business. Fitzgerald seems to be suggesting that although America has made a break with Europe, it still idealises the lifestyle of the European upper classes.

Tom is a snob. He says that Gatsby was too poor and lower class to be a suitable lover for Daisy: 'I'll be damned if I see how you got within a mile of her unless you brought the groceries to the back door' (p. 125). In fact, Gatsby came into contact with Daisy while he was training for war service, and during the war his bravery led to promotion to the rank of major.

Tom also calls into question Gatsby's reputation as 'an Oxford man' (p. 122). Gatsby's response is honest. He went to that prestigious English university for only five months, being offered the opportunity because of his service as an officer in the army. Nick admires Gatsby's honesty at this point: 'I had one of those renewals of complete faith in him that I'd experienced before'
(p. 123). Note however that in Chapter 8 we learn that, at the end of the war, Gatsby was desperate to return to America so he could be with Daisy; but 'some complication or misunderstanding sent him to Oxford instead' (p. 143).

GRADE BOOSTER **A02**

Although Nick Carraway is still narrating, this chapter makes extensive use of **dialogue** amongst the characters. Pay close attention to the ways in which dialogue, which may seem no more than small-talk, sheds light on the characters speaking. Tom speaks in a way that has a very different effect to the way Jordan speaks, for example. What they say may be trivial, but Fitzgerald is still developing our understanding of their characters.

REVISION FOCUS: TASK 6   A02

How far do you agree with the statements below?

● Daisy's character is revealed through the way she behaves with her daughter Pammy.
● Tom's character is revealed through his response to Gatsby's love for his wife Daisy.

Try writing opening paragraphs for essays based on the discussion points above. Set out your arguments clearly.

GLOSSARY

108	**Trimalchio** a wealthy patron and extravagant host in the *Satyricon*, a satirical work by the Roman author Petronius (died AD 65). For a while Fitzgerald wanted to call this novel, *Trimalchio in West Egg*
113	**blessed isles** in classical mythology, islands where eternal peace may be found
120	**mint julep** a drink made with bourbon whisky, sugar and mint, served with ice; very popular in the American South
121	**Louisville** the largest city in the state of Kentucky, named after King Louis XVI of France, a monarch beheaded in 1793 following the French Revolution. Louisville has been the location, since 1875, of the Kentucky Derby, the most popular American horse race
126	**Kapiolani … the Punch Bowl** parks in Honolulu, Hawaii, where the Buchanans spent their honeymoon

KEY QUOTATIONS: CHAPTER 7   A01

Key quotation 1: 'Her voice is full of money' (p. 115).

Possible interpretations:

- Daisy has the self-assurance that comes with wealth.
- Daisy is shallow and materialistic.
- Daisy belongs to a social class from which Gatsby remains excluded.

Key quotation 2: 'Mr Nobody from Nowhere' (p. 123).

Possible interpretations:

- Gatsby is socially unacceptable because he doesn't come from a well-established and wealthy family.
- Gatsby's background is mysterious, and perhaps sinister.
- Gatsby has erased his past and become free to take on a new identity.

CHECK THE BOOK   A03

Matthew J. Bruccoli's biography *Some Sort of Epic Grandeur: The Life of F. Scott Fitzgerald* (University of South Carolina Press, 2002) provides illuminating background information on the author of *The Great Gatsby*.

Other useful quotations:

- Daisy, regarding Gatsby: '"You resemble the advertisement of the man",' she went on innocently. '"You know the advertisement of the man –"' (p. 114)
- Tom, regarding Gatsby: '"I'll be damned if I see how you got within a mile of her unless you brought the groceries to the back door"' (p. 125)
- 'So we drove on toward death through the cooling twilight' (p. 129)

CHAPTER 8

SUMMARY

- After a sleepless night, Nick visits Gatsby as dawn approaches. Gatsby talks of his past, and of his love for Daisy, described as 'the following of a grail' (p. 142).
- Gatsby's gardener postpones draining the swimming pool, as Gatsby wants to use it.
- At noon, at work, Nick receives a call from Jordan Baker.
- George Wilson, grief-stricken at Myrtle's death, mistakes the eyes of Doctor T. J. Eckleburg on an advertising hoarding for the eyes of an all-seeing God.
- Wilson searches for the owner of the yellow car that killed his wife. He is directed to Gatsby, finds him floating in his swimming pool, and kills him. He then shoots himself.

ANALYSIS

ASHES TO ASHES, DUST TO DUST

Inside Gatsby's mansion Nick notices that now 'there was an inexplicable amount of dust everywhere' (p. 140). The word 'dust' should remind us of the description in Chapter 2 of George Wilson's home, in the valley of ashes, where 'a white ashen dust' covers everything (p. 28). Nick, Gatsby's neighbour, keeps Gatsby company at this difficult time; and Michaelis tries to look after his neighbour, George Wilson. Gatsby and Wilson are otherwise friendless men. At the end of this chapter, their separate lives converge, and both men die.

Note that in Chapter 1 Nick writes of the 'foul dust' that floated in the wake of Gatsby's dreams (p. 8). Note also that in Chapter 9 Tom, talking to Nick about Gatsby, says 'He threw dust into your eyes just like he did in Daisy's, but he was a tough one' (p. 169). Tom is alluding to the magic dust found in various legends and old stories which, when sprinkled in the eyes, induces sleep or dreams. But by this point in the novel, the association of dust and ashes with death has been firmly implanted in our minds.

IDENTITY

It was shortly before Gatsby's death that Nick actually found out the truth about him. He tells us that '"Jay Gatsby" had broken up like glass against Tom's hard malice' (p. 141). The new identity taken on by young James Gatz has been shattered, and it was at this point that Gatsby let Nick into the secret of his life-changing meetings with Dan Cody and with Daisy Fay.

Nick has already told us the story of Gatsby's life on Cody's yacht. He has saved the details about Gatsby's early encounters with Daisy until now. Nick's narration is skilfully structured in order to sustain a sense of mystery, while gradually revealing more and more about the reality behind Gatsby's image.

Mistaken identity plays a key role in the later chapters of this novel. Myrtle thinks that Tom, rather than Daisy is driving Gatsby's car. George Wilson believes that Gatsby has killed his wife, and in his grief he mistakes the eyes of Doctor T. J. Eckleburg on an advertising hoarding for the eyes of an all-seeing God.

CLASS

In Chapter 7, Tom snobbishly says to Gatsby, 'I'll be damned if I see how you got within a mile of her unless you brought the groceries to the back door' (p. 125). It is a spiteful comment, but it had an element of truth. Gatsby had met people of Daisy's social class before, 'but always with indiscernible barbed wire between' (p. 141). This 'barbed wire', figuratively keeping a distance between young Gatsby and the social elite, is a powerfully suggestive **metaphor**, given the use of barbed wire during the recent war in Europe.

Gatsby's sense of Daisy's social superiority, her wealth and 'comfortable family' (p. 142), makes explicit the class divisions within American society: 'Gatsby was overwhelmingly aware of the youth and mystery that wealth imprisons and preserves, of the freshness of many clothes, and of Daisy, gleaming like silver, safe and proud above the hot struggles of the poor' (p. 142). Equal opportunity is no longer a reality for Americans in the 1920s.

Daisy's family home in Louisville is described as a place that is at once 'cool' and 'radiant', a house that has 'a ripe mystery about it' (p. 141). In his own mansion, Gatsby has sought to capture that same sense of coolness, radiance and mystery, to make it attractive for Daisy.

THE KNIGHT IN THE PINK SUIT

Daisy became Gatsby's 'grail' (p. 142), the sacred object of his quest. His total devotion is reminiscent of the unswerving loyalty shown by knights in the medieval tales of King Arthur and his court. Gatsby is presented as a chivalrous hero whose shining armour takes the form of immaculate suits and shirts, whose trusty steed is his expensive automobile. Once again Old World values cast their long shadow across modern American realities.

> ## STUDY FOCUS: NOISES OFF A02
>
> Note the indirect way in which Fitzgerald presents Gatsby's death. A less skilful novelist might have resorted to melodramatic description. But Nick Carraway, our **narrator**, was not present to witness the killing at first hand, and the death of the novel's central character is rendered through shots reportedly heard by Gatsby's chauffeur. Look carefully at the steady build-up to this key incident. The pacing of **dialogue** in this chapter between the characters is particularly worthy of attention.

HOME SWEET HOME

Nick observes that Gatsby 'must have felt that he had lost the old warm world, paid a high price for living too long with a single dream' (p. 153). The 'old' world referred to here is not Europe but the Midwest, where Gatsby grew up. There is a verbal echo at this point of Nick's earlier remark that after the war the Midwest was no longer for him 'the warm centre of the world' (p. 9). Nick seems to miss the womb-like security of his childhood home. He has, of course, returned there in order to write his account of Gatsby's life.

Gatsby made a deliberate break with the past and has tried to make a fresh start. But by the end of his life, Nick suggests, this 'new world' of Gatsby's own making has become a strange and unsettling place, lit by 'raw' sunlight: 'A new world, material without being real, where poor ghosts, breathing dreams like air, drifted fortuitously about ... like that ashen, fantastic figure gliding toward him through the amorphous trees' (pp. 153–4). That figure belongs to George Wilson, who is about to kill Jay Gatsby.

GLOSSARY	
143	**'Beale Street Blues'** jazz tune written in 1917 by W. C. Handy (1873–1958), known as 'the Father of the Blues'
147	**Hempstead ... Southampton** towns on Long Island, New York

> **CONTEXT** A04
>
> The Holy Grail was the cup from which Jesus Christ drank at the Last Supper. It was used by Joseph of Arimathea to catch Christ's blood during the Crucifixion. The quest for the Grail later became a major **narrative** element in legends of King Arthur and his court, found notably in *Le Morte d'Arthur* [The Death of Arthur] (1485) by Sir Thomas Malory (1405–71). Sir Galahad was the knight who led the quest for this sacred vessel.

CHAPTER 9

SUMMARY

- Nick makes the arrangements for Gatsby's funeral.
- The Buchanans have left New York, leaving no contact address.
- Nick visits Meyer Wolfshiem, who says he is unable to attend the funeral.
- One of the few mourners present is Henry C. Gatz, who has travelled from the Midwest, after reading of Gatsby's death in a Chicago newspaper. He speaks with pride of his son's attainments.
- Later in the year, Nick bumps into Tom Buchanan, who admits telling George Wilson that it was Gatsby's car which killed Myrtle.
- The novel ends with Nick contemplating the empty mansion, and pondering the significance of Gatsby's story.

GRADE BOOSTER **A01**

The Great Gatsby is not a long novel but it is written in a very concentrated way, and reveals more each time you read it. Once you have grasped the basic story, pay attention to the way it is told. Characters will appear in a different light on second or third reading. It will enhance your grade if your answer shows that rereading has deepened your understanding of the book.

ANALYSIS

THE SCENE OF THE CRIME

Note the vocabulary Nick uses when describing the aftermath of Gatsby's murder. The words 'adventitious' (meaning incidental) and 'pasquinade' (meaning a lampoon or parody) leap out as unfamiliar words. Such vocabulary seems to have been chosen to keep us at a distance from the crime scene.

You might expect that this description of a crime scene, complete with police investigators and news reporters, would include a degree of sensationalism. But there is a kind of protective formality in Nick's use of such words, as though he wants to shield his neighbour from the effects of gossip and lurid reporting. We are not led to feel like onlookers, gawping at the scene; rather, we are made aware of the presence of Nick, our careful **narrator**.

FRIENDS AND NEIGHBOURS

In this final chapter, Nick emphasises Gatsby's isolation. After hosting all those lavish parties, it turns out that he was essentially alone all the time. Nick has only known Gatsby for three months at the time of his death, yet it is left to him to arrange the funeral. Owl Eyes attends the ceremony, yet he never really knew Gatsby at all. His presence seems random, and that makes Gatsby's aloneness seem still more complete.

We might conclude that Gatsby deserved to be so isolated; it is the price he paid for 'living too long with a single dream' (p. 153). Up to this point we have been led to understand that Gatsby totally erased his past, left his parents behind and had no further contact with them. But Nick now reveals that Gatsby has in fact sent his father, Henry C. Gatz, a photograph of his mansion. He has, moreover, visited his father and bought him a house too. Henry C. Gatz is proud of his son and says, 'ever since he made a success he was very generous with me' (p. 164).

Is this true, or is the old man deluding himself? Henry C. Gatz seems an honest man, whose word we ought to trust. The well-worn photograph he carries also suggests that he is telling the truth. Remember that ever since this funeral Nick has been aware of Gatz's claim that his son kept in touch and was good to him. Yet all through the narration so far he has led us to believe that Gatsby simply turned his back on his parents. Introducing this sense that the break with his past wasn't total, Nick now makes Gatsby seem more human, less aloof and more deserving of his and our own sympathy.

REVISION FOCUS: TASK 7   **A02**

How far do you agree with the statements below?

● Jay Gatsby was 'great' because he stood apart from the crowd.

● The presence of Henry C. Gatz makes Jay Gatsby seem more human.

Try writing opening paragraphs for essays based on the discussion points above. Set out your arguments clearly.

A STORY OF THE WEST

We have noticed how, from the outset, this novel located in New York, on America's East coast, has made extensive use of the American West's long association with new beginnings and unlimited potential. Nick now talks of growing up in the Midwest, not on the West coast but in the physical heart of the American republic. He remembers going home from school and from college, and associates the Middle West with 'the thrilling returning trains of my youth' (p. 167). As a boy and young man, he found the westward journey exhilarating, but note that he was returning to the bosom of his family, rather than heading out for some unexplored and unsettled wilderness.

At this point he realises that 'this has been a story of the West, after all' (p. 167). The European settlement of America started on the East coast and moved steadily across the continent to the West coast. But the characters in this book have moved in the opposite direction – from America's cosy Middle to its exciting and energetic East – and Nick suggests that their solid, comfortable upbringing didn't prepare them for the more dynamic and competitive conditions of life in New York.

After Gatsby's death, Nick says that life in the East seemed to be 'distorted beyond my eyes' power of correction' (p. 167). Vision is an important theme in *The Great Gatsby*. This theme covers issues ranging from the difficulty of making a clear-sighted interpretation of events to the power of seeing beyond immediate circumstances, using the visionary capacity of hope and imagination. Does Nick really prefer to see things as they are? Or would he prefer to see things as they might become?

CONTEXT   **A04**

Nick compares West Egg after Gatsby's death to 'a night scene by El Greco' (p. 167). El Greco (1541–1614) was a Spanish painter of religious scenes whose figures tended to seem elongated and oddly distorted.

STUDY FOCUS: A SHARED DEFICIENCY   **A02**

Nick tells us that he 'began to have a feeling of defiance, of scornful solidarity between Gatsby and me against them all' (p. 157). Ten pages later, however, he identifies himself not just with Gatsby, but also with Tom, Daisy and Jordan. They are all Midwesterners, and 'perhaps had some deficiency in common which made us subtly unadaptable to Eastern life' (p. 167). Nick's narration is the means by which we get to know all these characters. But can you identify attitudes or characteristics he shares with all four?

GLOSSARY

160   **James J. Hill** (1838–1916) a powerful businessman, who rose from humble origins. He ran the Great Northern Railway, which was based in St Paul (the city where Fitzgerald was born)

Greenwich a suburb of New York City

161   **The Swastika Holding Company** the swastika, formerly a symbol of good fortune in India, was adopted by Hitler's anti-semitic Nazi party in Germany in 1920

'The Rosary' a song written in 1898, popular in the 1920s

162   **the American Legion** an organisation for veterans of the US armed forces, formed in 1919

EXTENDED COMMENTARY

CHAPTER 9, PP. 170–2

This passage is pervaded by a sense of things coming to an end; it has an air of finality. The word 'last' occurs three times on p. 171. The party is over in a literal and a **metaphorical** sense, and Nick is preparing to leave the bustling, energetic East for the quiet, reflective Midwest. But his departure is followed by a new beginning. Two years after returning home, Nick will write this account, living through the experiences of that summer once again in his memory and imagination, as he carefully composes his book. In a sense, Nick has brought Jay Gatsby, his former neighbour, back to life through the preceding pages, and has transformed himself; this worker in the world of finance has become a creative writer of prose.

Light plays an important role throughout *The Great Gatsby*: the green light at the end of Daisy's dock; the blaze of electric lighting at Gatsby's parties; the glare of the hot sun in Chapter 7. Fitzgerald understood well how our perception of things can change according to changes in the light, and in *The Great Gatsby* he makes light itself an important component in the narrative. The end of the novel is illuminated by moonlight. The world seen by moonlight can appear very different to the brightly lit world of daytime, and it is fitting that the closing pages of *The Great Gatsby* should be bathed in this more mysterious kind of light. Fitzgerald's book mixes **realism** with **romance**.

The term 'romance' is often used to indicate a love story. Fitzgerald's book is certainly that. But romance has a more specialised meaning, defined helpfully by an earlier

American writer, Nathaniel Hawthorne (1804–64). In 'The Custom-House,' an introductory essay to his own romance *The Scarlet Letter* (1850), Hawthorne wrote:

Moonlight, in a familiar room, falling so white upon the carpet, and showing all its figures so distinctly, – making every object so minutely visible, yet so unlike a morning or noontide visibility, – is a medium the most suitable for a romance-writer to get acquainted with his illusive guests … the floor of our familiar room has become a neutral territory, somewhere between the real world and fairy-land, where the Actual and the Imaginary may meet, and each imbue itself with the nature of the other.

CONTEXT **A04**

Maxwell Perkins (1884–1947) was a famous American literary editor, who in 1919 'discovered' F. Scott Fitzgerald for the New York publishing house, Charles Scribner's Sons. The support and constructive criticism that Perkins gave Fitzgerald helped him to achieve his finest work, *The Great Gatsby*.

This classic passage may help you to understand more fully the kind of book that Fitzgerald has written. The world of romance, located 'somewhere between the real world and fairy-land', is a suitable place to find Jay Gatsby, who in Chapter 6 is said to believe that 'the rock of the world was founded securely on a fairy's wing' (p. 96).

In the aftermath of Gatsby's death, the moon illuminates an obscene word that some boy has written on one of the steps of Gatsby's mansion. Nick erases the scrawl, already guarding Jay Gatsby's memory against other people's words. Nick also makes reference in this passage to a taxi driver, who pauses as he passes Gatsby's house in order to share with passengers his own version of events. The taxi driver knows that people tend to love gossip, especially if it has an element of scandal. Myrtle Wilson loved to read such stories in the magazine *Town Tattle*. Nick clearly wants to prevent that kind of tattle after Gatsby's death, and he writes his book caringly, to set the record straight.

Initially, Fitzgerald placed the reference to Dutch sailors encountering the New World at the end of Chapter 1, but in the course of writing this novel he shifted it to the end, where it provides a resonant and memorable conclusion.

Fitzgerald suggests that America (for Old World settlers, not for the Native Americans they removed or displaced) was founded on 'a transitory enchanted moment' when a newly arrived European came 'face to face for the last time in history with something commensurate to his capacity for wonder' (p. 171). America is a physical place; yet its history has been fuelled by dreams. Is Fitzgerald suggesting that the dreams upon which the American republic was founded have been betrayed by its historical reality? Is he suggesting that America, like Gatsby's house after his death, now appears to be 'a huge incoherent failure' (p. 171)?

The final paragraphs strongly convey the irreversible passing of time. The Dutch sailors, who arrived on this coast and were astonished at what they found, are long gone. The trees that once grew there have made way for Gatsby's house, and now Gatsby himself has gone. Does America remain a land of promise, or has its potential been exhausted?

The narrative focus narrows from 'the fresh, green breast of the new world' to 'the green light' at the end of the Buchanans' dock (p. 171). Nick contemplates the failure of Gatsby's dream, and identifies the green light with 'the orgastic future that year by year recedes before us' (p. 171). 'Orgastic' is another example of Nick's taste for obscure words. It looks like 'orgiastic', meaning riotous or indulgent, and might seem to refer back to the wild parties that Gatsby hosted.

But when his editor, Maxwell Perkins, queried the word 'orgastic', F. Scott Fitzgerald explained that it was an adjective from 'orgasm', an alternative version of orgasmic, and that it was intended to express a state of ecstasy. Orgasm, as a culminating moment of sexual excitement, suggests intense experience which seems to stand outside the flow of historical time. Gatsby's dream of Daisy seems to have been not just erotic, but ecstatic – he was less concerned with her physical reality, than with clinging on to that feeling of standing outside of historical time that he experienced at the moment of falling in love with her.

Falling in love seems to have made Gatsby feel immortal. Now, however, he is dead, and his story is told by Nick, who at thirty is very conscious of growing older. Remember that James Gatz 'invented just the sort of Jay Gatsby that a seventeen-year-old boy would be likely to invent, and to this conception he was faithful to the end' (p. 95). Gatsby was imagined by a boy on the verge of becoming an adult. Adulthood, however, teaches us that we are not immortal, that we cannot live forever in moments of intensity and enchantment. Time passes: 'So we beat on, boats against the current, borne back ceaselessly into the past' (p. 172).

CONTEXT **A04**

In the early seventeenth century, a territory called New Netherland was established by Dutch colonisers on the East coast of America. The main settlement in this territory, called New Amsterdam, was founded in 1625, at the southern tip of Manhattan. The region passed into English ownership in 1674, and New Amsterdam came to be known as New York.

CHARACTERS

JAY GATSBY

WHO IS JAY GATSBY?

- A wealthy, glamorous and mysterious figure, who throws lavish parties at his mansion in Long Island, New York.
- A Midwestern youth called James Gatz, who has reinvented himself.
- A man who seems to embody idealistic love, but in fact has close connections with the criminal underworld.

NICK CARRAWAY'S NEIGHBOUR

Jay Gatsby is Nick Carraway's neighbour, in West Egg village, Long Island. Nick, our **narrator**, lives in a small house; Gatsby has a huge mansion set in an enormous garden. He is attended by servants, owns expensive cars, motorboats and a hydroplane. Gatsby regularly throws lavish parties, with fine food and drink and music for dancing.

Before Nick meets Gatsby he imagines him to be 'a florid and corpulent person in his middle years.' (p. 50). In fact, he is a year or two over thirty, sun-tanned and handsome with short hair, well groomed and immaculately dressed. Although he is an extravagantly generous host, he drinks very little and keeps himself apart, almost an onlooker at his own parties.

MR NOBODY FROM NOWHERE

Gatsby's background is a mystery. Tom Buchanan calls him 'Mr Nobody from Nowhere' (p. 123). Because not much is known about Gatsby, there is a lot of gossip about him. He is said to have attended Oxford University. A common rumour suggests that he has killed a man. There is also speculation that was a German spy, working for the enemy during the First World War, and that he is related to the German ruler Kaiser Wilhelm II. These rumours suggest, perhaps, that Gatsby's physical appearance is Germanic. Nick has discovered some details of Gatsby's actual background, and as he narrates this story he gradually discloses more and more of the facts that lie behind Gatsby's image as a man of mystery.

CONTEXT A04

Today, nearly a fifth of the American population can claim German ancestry. A particularly high concentration of these German Americans live in Midwestern states such as North Dakota.

STUDY FOCUS: THE TERMS OF GREATNESS A02

The title *The Great Gatsby* prepares us, as readers, for the story of an exceptional man. Think carefully about elements of his story that show Gatsby to be in some sense 'great'. Pay attention too to character flaws that suggest just the opposite of 'greatness'. Remember that Nick, our narrator, is the lens through which we see Gatsby. Is it a distorting lens or can we trust the image of Gatsby that eventually appears within Nick's account? What are we to make of Nick's assessment that 'Gatsby turned out all right at the end' (p. 8)?

FROM GATZ TO GATSBY

James Gatz grew up in North Dakota, in America's Midwest, the son of unsuccessful farm people. At seventeen he changed his name to Jay Gatsby. As a boy he explored the shores of Lake Superior, becoming physically fit and getting to know the natural world in that area. This enabled him to warn Dan Cody that his yacht was moored in a potentially dangerous place. Cody, who had grown rich prospecting for precious metals, became a kind of surrogate father for Gatsby. Following Cody's death, Gatsby became involved with the gambler Meyer Wolfshiem, a shady and sinister figure from the underworld of organised crime. Wolfshiem not only describes Gatsby as 'a perfect gentleman' and 'a man of fine breeding', but he suggests that he is 'the kind of man you'd like to take home and introduce to your mother and sister' (p. 70). Gatsby clearly has charm, an element of charisma. Nick notices especially that he has 'one of those rare smiles with a quality of eternal reassurance in it' (p. 49).

MAKING GATSBY GREAT

Gatsby takes great pains to present himself as a gentleman and a man of breeding. He owns a Rolls-Royce car and has his clothes bought at expensive shops in London. He habitually uses the term 'old sport', a phrase intended to make him seem upper class. Gatsby is acting out a role, and Nick indicates that he is trying a little too hard, that his 'elaborate formality of speech just missed being absurd' (p. 49). In his mansion, Gatsby has a library with English oak panelling, designed to resemble one you might find in an Oxford college. The character Owl Eyes, who doesn't really know Gatsby at all, is hugely impressed by the realistic appearance of the library; although he notes that the pages of the books remain uncut, and are unread. Gatsby aims to project the image of an Old World aristocrat. He actually comes across as an extravagant, yet very thorough New World showman.

THE WAR

We are told that Gatsby 'did extraordinarily well in the war' (p. 143). His brave conduct during the conflict resulted in promotion to the rank of major. This enhanced his social status, and seems to have made it easier for him to make useful connections. A scheme that enabled American officers to attend European universities also led to him spending five months at Oxford.

Seen from another angle, however, the war was disastrous for Gatsby. As a young lieutenant, before leaving to fight in France, he met Daisy Fay in Louisville, Kentucky and fell head over heels in love. During his absence overseas Daisy met and married Tom Buchanan. The conduct of Gatsby's life from that moment had a single goal – to win back Daisy's love and to take her away from her husband. The intensity of that obsession separates Gatsby from the crowd; he is a man driven by desire, and his life has purpose. But that obsession leads to his downfall.

IMAGE AND REALITY

Gatsby presents himself as a wealthy American who doesn't need to work. But as Nick remarks, young men didn't just 'drift coolly out of nowhere and buy a palace on Long Island Sound' (p. 50). In three years, Gatsby had made the money to buy this luxurious mansion. He did so through the criminal activity of bootlegging, supplying alcoholic drink illegally. His close involvement with Wolfshiem suggests that he has taken part in other illicit activities. Gatsby acts out the role of a sophisticated man of the world, yet when he meets Daisy again after five years apart he is overcome with embarrassment and nervousness; Nick actually tells him, 'You're acting like a little boy' (p. 85). The fact is, when James Gatz changed his name 'he invented just the sort of Jay Gatsby that a seventeen-year-old boy would be likely to invent, and to this conception he was faithful to the end' (p. 95).

CONTEXT · A04

Owl Eyes compares Gatsby to David Belasco (1853–1931), a New York theatre producer renowned for paying close attention to realistic details on the stage. Belasco is said to have been so painstaking that once when he needed a restaurant setting he bought a real one and had it moved to the theatre and reassembled on stage. He was also renowned for his spectacular use of new lighting techniques.

KEY QUOTATION: JAY GATSBY

Key quotation: Gatsby has 'an extraordinary gift for hope' (p. 8).

Possible interpretations:

- Gatsby is able to imagine a life that fulfils his dreams.
- Hope is a positive quality in a society as well as in an individual.
- Gatsby's commitment to the future puts him out of touch with the present.

NICK CARRAWAY

WHO IS NICK?

- The narrator of *The Great Gatsby*.
- A distant relative of Daisy, and Gatsby's next-door neighbour.
- A worker in the world of finance, who returns to the Midwest and becomes a writer.

THE MIDWEST AND THE WIDER WORLD

Nick Carraway's family run a hardware business and have become well-to-do. Nick grew up in a Midwestern city. He has returned there after working in finance in New York City, on the East coast. Before entering the financial world, Nick had graduated from Yale University. He had also served in the American army, in France, in the First World War.

A LITERARY MAN

Nick tells us that he was 'rather literary in college' (p. 10). Now he is the **narrator** of this story, as well as a character in it. In fact, he tells us he is actually writing the book we are reading. So we come to know Nick's character in part through his literary style and his use of language. What he writes about is revealing; we need to ask why he is so interested in Jay Gatsby. But we can also learn things about Nick by paying attention to the way he writes. The things we learn don't always seem to fit comfortably with what he tells us about himself.

Nick is well educated, so he occasionally uses obscure words. It is surprising, however, that a worker in finance, from a family in the hardware business, should have such a poetic and lyrical style. Nick presents himself as a dull and ordinary individual, but his writing discloses a passionate and imaginative nature, despite his outwardly reserved demeanour.

MELANCHOLY

Nick seems to find the world a sad place, and he has the verbal skills to express that, 'At the enchanted metropolitan twilight I felt a haunting loneliness sometimes, and felt it in others' (p. 57). He gets melancholy when he contemplates growing old. Although only thirty, he looks forward bleakly to 'the promise of a decade of loneliness, a thinning list of single men to know, a thinning brief-case of enthusiasm, thinning hair' (p. 129).

CONTEXT **A04**

Yale University, in New Haven, Connecticut, was founded in 1701. It is the third oldest higher educational establishment in America. It is noted for its campus architecture in the Gothic Revival style, like Gatsby's library (which, we are told, is actually modelled on one at Merton College Oxford).

GRADE BOOSTER **A02**

What does 'reserving judgements' actually involve, in Nick's case? It may help to bear in mind Nick's later description of himself as 'within and without, simultaneously enchanted and repelled by the inexhaustible variety of life' (p. 37). He seems to place himself on the threshold of the action, at once part of it and apart from it.

STUDY FOCUS: RESERVING JUDGEMENTS **A02**

At the start of the book, Nick tells us, 'I'm inclined to reserve all judgements'. He then adds, 'Reserving judgements is a matter of infinite hope' (p. 7). This is a quotation that is worth bearing in mind as you follow his narration. Nick is attracted to Gatsby's 'extraordinary gift for hope' (p. 8), but Gatsby's belief in the possibility of regaining Daisy's love seems rather different from the kind of hope you experience when you hold back from passing judgement on someone or something.

KEY QUOTATION: NICK CARRAWAY **A01**

Key quotation: 'I liked to walk up Fifth Avenue and pick out romantic women from the crowd and imagine that in a few minutes I was going to enter into their lives, and no one would ever know or disapprove.' (p. 57)

Possible interpretations:

- Nick tends to see other people as supporting characters in his own life-story.
- Our knowledge of Jay Gatsby is deeply coloured by Nick's romantic imagination.

DAISY BUCHANAN (NÉE FAY)

WHO IS DAISY?

- Nick Carraway's second cousin once removed.
- Tom Buchanan's wife.
- The woman Jay Gatsby loves.

THE MOST POPULAR GIRL IN LOUISVILLE

Daisy Fay grew up in a wealthy family in Louisville, Kentucky, in the American Midwest. Jordan Baker says that Daisy, who dressed in white and drove a white car, was 'by far the most popular of all the young girls in Louisville' (pp. 72–3). She is also said to have been popular in Chicago, after her marriage to Tom Buchanan. Yet at the time of the novel's action, Daisy's social life seems to have grown narrow. She never attends Gatsby's parties, so he has to contrive a meeting with her over tea at Nick Carraway's house.

DAISY'S VOICE

Daisy's maiden name Fay suggests that she has Irish ancestry, but 'fay' is also an old English word for fairy and Gatsby has obviously fallen under her spell. The name Daisy itself suggests a delicate flower. She has 'dark shining hair' (p. 143).

Nick clearly finds her very attractive: 'Her face was sad and lovely with bright things in it ... but there was an excitement in her voice that men who had cared for her found difficult to forget' (p. 14). Does this insight imply that Nick himself has 'cared for' this young woman? He is always responsive to that voice, 'with its fluctuating, feverish warmth' (p. 93). When she finally attends one of Gatsby's parties and begins to sing along with the music, Nick comments on her 'husky, rhythmic whisper' (p. 104). Note though that Gatsby bluntly says, 'Her voice is full of money' (p. 115). Her voice obviously registered her family's wealth and made him conscious of his own lack of money when he first met her.

DAISY AS A MOTHER

Daisy, who is in her early twenties, has a three-year-old daughter, named Pammy. The child is looked after by a nanny, and during the one scene where we see mother and daughter together Daisy's response to Pammy seems shallow and inadequate. More generally, Daisy's conversation seems superficial, and sometimes rather stupid. She admits to being cynical, and Nick describes her as unthoughtful and insincere.

STUDY FOCUS: A BEAUTIFUL LITTLE FOOL A02

Thinking about her daughter Pammy's future, Daisy says, '- that's the best thing a girl can be in this world, a beautiful little fool' (p. 22). Does that description fit Daisy's character? Or, are there respects in which Daisy seems worthy of Gatsby's devotion?

KEY QUOTATION: DAISY BUCHANAN A01

Key quotation: 'I've been everywhere and seen everything and done everything' (p. 22).

Possible interpretations:

- Daisy belongs to a wealthy and privileged social class.
- Daisy's understanding of life is very superficial.
- Daisy has nothing left to hope for and nothing to give her a sense of purpose.

CONTEXT **A04**

Polo is sometimes known as 'the Sport of Kings'. It is played by two teams of four on horseback. The aim is to drive a small, hard ball into the opposition's goal, using a long wooden mallet. Polo was first played in America in 1876.

TOM BUCHANAN

WHO IS TOM?

- A man who has inherited wealth and is descended from the Scottish gentry.
- He is married to Daisy, but also has an affair with Myrtle Wilson.
- Nick knew him at Yale University, where Tom excelled at American football.

A CRUEL BODY

Tom Buchanan is 'a sturdy straw-haired man of thirty, with a rather hard mouth and a supercilious manner' (p. 12). He walks in an 'alert, aggressive way' (p. 169). His eyes are described as shining, arrogant and restless and his body is muscular and very powerful. Nick sums it up as 'a cruel body' (p. 12). Tom comes from an 'enormously wealthy' Midwestern family (p. 11). He likes to display his wealth, and when he moved to East Egg, he brought a team of polo ponies with him. Tom acknowledges that he is not a popular man.

A SIMPLE MIND

Nick knew Tom at Yale University, where Tom excelled at American football, rather than in the classroom. Nick now says that Tom has 'a simple mind' (p. 119). In contrast to Gatsby, who has 'an extraordinary gift for hope' (p. 8), Tom is pessimistic about the future. He fears that civilization is on the verge of collapse, and he holds racist views. Tom refers to books in which he has read the latest scientific theories, but when he refers to them it is clear that he is simply drawn to ideas that seem to support his pessimistic outlook, and that his understanding of science is very limited (see pp. 18, 112 and 116).

STUDY FOCUS: RACIST VIEWS A04

Tom makes several racist comments, including the dramatic declaration: 'It's up to us, who are the dominant race, to watch out or these other races will have control of things' (p. 18). Is racism a character flaw specific to Tom in this novel, or does Fitzgerald present a broader picture of racist attitudes in America?

ADULTERY

Since the early days of his marriage to Daisy, Tom has had affairs with other women. Throughout the novel he commits adultery with Myrtle Wilson, a working-class woman married to a garage mechanic. Tom uses Myrtle in a cynical way, buying her presents but telling her lies, and when she drunkenly repeats Daisy's name he breaks her nose.

Despite his long-term involvement with mistresses, Tom becomes very moralistic when he feels threatened by Gatsby's love for Daisy. His outburst is hypocritical and characteristically racist: 'Nowadays people begin by sneering at family life and family institutions, and next they'll throw everything overboard and have marriage between black and white' (p. 124).

KEY QUOTATION: TOM BUCHANAN A01

Key quotation: Tom at Yale: 'a national figure in a way, one of those men who reach such an acute limited excellence at twenty-one that everything afterward savours of anti-climax' (p. 11).

Possible interpretations:

- Tom's life has peaked too early, and his limited celebrity has faded.
- Tom's personality is an example of arrested development.

Jordan Baker

Who is Jordan Baker?

- A golfing celebrity, said to have cheated in a major tournament.
- Daisy's bridesmaid.
- A close friend of Nick.

A modern woman

Jordan Baker is a couple of years younger than Daisy. They grew up together in Louisville, Kentucky, and when Daisy married Tom Buchanan, Jordan acted as her bridesmaid. On the East coast, Jordan lives with her aunt.

Jordan is a slender, sun-tanned young woman with grey eyes and an upright posture. Her hair is said to be 'the colour of an autumn leaf' (p. 168). Nick sums her up as 'this clean, hard, limited person, who dealt in universal scepticism' (p. 77). He tells us that she has a 'bored haughty face' (p. 58) and a 'scornful mouth' (p. 78). Such description presents Jordan in a negative light, especially as she is only in her early twenties, but Nick is attracted to her nonetheless and there are clear indications that they have become more intimately involved than he openly lets on.

Study focus: This hard, clean, limited person | A02

Why should Jordan, who is clearly attractive, young and talented be so cynical, bored and scornful? Nick tells us a certain amount about her, but there seems to be much more to her story. Why is she living with her aunt? What actually happened in the golf tournament where she was accused of cheating? Nick fills in details of Gatsby's background, but think carefully about how much he lets us know about the other characters in this novel. Are we led to suspect that Nick knows more about Jordan than he shares with us?

Sport and celebrity

Jordan is a professional celebrity sportswoman, and she is physically sporty. Nick admires the 'jauntiness' of her movements, 'as if she had first learned to walk upon golf courses on clean, crisp mornings' (pp. 51–2). But when Nick witnesses Jordan telling a lie, he recalls a rumour that she has cheated in a golf tournament, creating a scandal. Note how Nick, who prides himself on his ability to reserve judgement, makes the shocking declaration, 'She was incurably dishonest' (p. 58). Is Nick being fair to Jordan here?

Key quotation: Jordan Baker | A01

Key quotation: Jordan to Nick: 'I thought you were rather an honest, straightforward person. I thought it was your secret pride' (p. 168).

Possible interpretations:

- Jordan seems resilient, but here she shows herself to be emotionally vulnerable.
- Neither Jordan nor Nick are good at sustaining romantic relationships.
- Despite her apparent cynicism, Jordan actually values honesty and straightforwardness.

CONTEXT | A04

The 1920s was a decade when young women, often known as 'flappers', exercised unprecedented freedom. They had their hair cut short, wore relatively short skirts and used make-up to make themselves more attractive. It was Fitzgerald, in his short stories, who introduced this newly liberated woman into literature. Jordan is not a 'flapper', simply having a wild time, but she is clearly a thoroughly modern young woman, independent and aware of the ways of the world.

GEORGE AND MYRTLE WILSON

WHO ARE THE WILSONS?

- George Wilson is a mechanic, who runs a garage; Myrtle is his wife.
- Myrtle is Tom Buchanan's mistress.
- George kills Gatsby after his car, actually driven by Daisy, has killed Myrtle.

VALLEY OF ASHES

George Wilson runs a garage in the bleak, dust-covered 'valley of ashes' (p. 26), a spot half-way between West Egg and New York where the city's waste is dumped. George is described as 'a blond, spiritless man, anaemic and faintly handsome' (pp. 26–7). His neighbour, Michaelis also recognises that spiritless quality, and sees him as 'one of these worn-out men'. He adds that George is 'his wife's man and not his own' (p. 130). Tom Buchanan's dismissive judgement is that George is 'so dumb he doesn't know he's alive' (p. 29). After Myrtle's death George kills Gatsby before taking his own life.

A RICH MAN'S WORLD

Myrtle Wilson is Tom Buchanan's mistress. She is in her mid-thirties, a few years older than Tom, full-figured and sensual, unlike Daisy who seems to be physically delicate. Seeing Myrtle, Nick remarks that 'there was an immediately perceptible vitality about her as if the nerves of her body were continually smouldering' (p. 28).

Since her marriage, twelve years earlier, Myrtle has helped run the garage. With Tom she is given a glimpse of another world, a world of wealth and leisure. At the apartment, Myrtle puts on ridiculous airs and graces and her laughter is described as 'artificial' (p. 38). She tries to live out the role of a rich man's wife, but then she has to return to her husband and their dismal home above the garage. Tom is determined to keep it that way.

CRITICAL VIEWPOINT A02

There is an unlikely parallel between Myrtle glimpsing a previously unknown world in Tom's lifestyle and Gatsby discovering a new world in Daisy Fay's family background. Both Myrtle and Gatsby are outsiders, from the lower social class, and both are dazzled by wealth and glamour that they want to make their own. Gatsby sends a photo of his house to Henry C. Gatz; Myrtle places her mother's photo on the wall on the apartment.

STUDY FOCUS: PARENTS AND CHILDREN A02

Myrtle Wilson has a photograph of her mother on the wall of the apartment that Tom keeps for their extra-marital affair. She also plans to buy a wreath for her mother's grave. Myrtle seems devoted to her mother's memory. What light does that devotion shed on the relationship of parents and their children in *The Great Gatsby*?

Myrtle met Tom on a train and was dazzled by the clothes he wore. This may remind us of Daisy's response to Gatsby's 'beautiful shirts' (see p. 89). Myrtle was dismayed to find out that George borrowed the suit he wore at their wedding. She says she married him because she thought he was a gentleman, but discovered 'he wasn't fit to lick my shoe' (p. 36). However, her involvement with Tom is her first extra-marital affair. Was she still in love with George when this new world opened up for her? The reality of this new world is made clear when Tom breaks Myrtle's nose merely because she drunkenly repeats Daisy's name.

KEY QUOTATION: GEORGE WILSON A01

Key quotation: '"God sees everything," repeated Wilson' (p. 152).

Possible interpretations:

- The strength of George Wilson's feelings for Myrtle leaves him mentally unstable after her death.
- In this materialistic society, only a man who is mentally ill expresses belief in God.
- God may be all-seeing, but the man George Wilson murders was not the driver of the car that killed Myrtle.

MEYER WOLFSHIEM

WHO IS MEYER WOLFSHIEM?

- The man who fixed the baseball World Series in 1919.
- One of Gatsby's close associates from the criminal underworld.
- A man who is both sentimental and ruthless.

THE CRIMINAL UNDERWORLD

Nick Carraway meets Meyer Wolfshiem at lunch with Gatsby, in Chapter 4. Wolfshiem, fifty years old, is described as 'a small, flat-nosed Jew' with a 'large head' and 'tiny eyes' (p. 68). He recalls people he has known, now 'dead and gone' (p. 68), presumably killed by gangsters. He looks around him apprehensively, inspecting the people in the restaurant, clearly nervous that he might be in danger from some enemy in the world of organised crime.

Wolfshiem wears cuff buttons made from human teeth. This suggests a sinister, even cruel side to Wolfshiem's character, yet his eyes regularly fill with tears. Gatsby says of Wolfshiem, 'He becomes very sentimental sometimes' (p. 71). At such moments he appears soft hearted, but beneath the surface he is a ruthless criminal. Wolfshiem sums up Gatsby's qualities by saying 'There's the kind of man you'd like to take home and introduce to your mother and sister' (p. 70). But remember that Wolfshiem introduces Gatsby not to his mother and sister but to connections in the criminal underworld.

CHECK THE BOOK A03

Arnold Rothstein, the real-life gangster on whom Meyer Wolfshiem is modelled, was also the inspiration for Nathan Detroit, a character in Damon Runyon's 1933 short story 'The Idyll of Miss Sarah Brown'. That story was the basis for the famous musical *Guys and Dolls*.

STUDY FOCUS: ETHNIC ORIGINS   A02

Wolfshiem is Jewish. Fitzgerald has him say 'Oggsford' for Oxford, to indicate that he has a distinctive accent (p. 70). Pay close attention to issues of race in *The Great Gatsby*. In a land of equal opportunity, it is clear that certain racial groups are disadvantaged and that family background and ethnic origins play an important role. Wolfshiem has become wealthy, but crime has been his route.

GATSBY'S SECOND MENTOR?

Tom Buchanan alleges that Wolfshiem and Gatsby bought up a lot of general stores and used them to sell alcohol illegally. Nick wonders whether Gatsby too was involved in fixing the 1919 baseball World Series, that major betrayal of the trust of American sports fans. After Gatsby's death, Wolfshiem tells Nick that he actually 'made' Gatsby the man he was: 'I raised him up out of nothing, right out of the gutter' (p. 162). We know that Gatsby inherited no money from Dan Cody, so it is possible that Wolfshiem is telling the truth about the key role he played in his acquisition of wealth.

When Daisy starts to visit Gatsby's house, he dismisses his servants, to prevent gossip. In their place he hires people supplied by Wolfshiem; these associates of a gangster have been trained to keep quiet. Gatsby's chauffeur, 'one of Wolfshiem's protégés' (p. 154), hears the shots fired by George Wilson but doesn't take much notice of them. The implication is that gunshots are not unfamiliar to a man used to living in Wolfshiem's social circle.

KEY QUOTATION: MEYER WOLFSHIEM   A01

Key quotation: Gatsby of Wolfshiem: 'He's the man who fixed the World's Series back in 1919' (p. 71).

Possible interpretations:

- Gatsby's closest friends are gangsters.
- Desire for wealth, or greed, is pervasive in Fitzgerald's America.

THEMES

AMERICAN IDEALS

UNDER THE RED, WHITE, AND BLUE

For a while, Fitzgerald planned to call this book *Under the Red, White, and Blue*. That title invokes the 'Stars and Stripes', the national flag, as an emblem of American ideals.

The American literary critic Lionel Trilling (1905–75) argued that, in a sense, Gatsby *is* America. His character embodies key aspects of the nation's dreams and realities.

As well as telling the story of a glamorous individual, Fitzgerald is addressing the fate of American ideals during a period when the hopes and aspirations expressed in the Declaration of Independence, back in 1776, were being put under pressure or distorted by the materialism, consumerism and violent rivalry of early twentieth-century life.

John Dos Passos (1896–1970), one of the major novelists amongst Fitzgerald's contemporaries, was also disturbed by what he saw as twentieth-century America's abandonment of its fundamental values and founding ideals. His brilliant novel *Manhattan Transfer* (1925) depicts a society where a vast gap has opened between rich and poor and where mean self-interest governs people's actions.

EQUALITY OF OPPORTUNITY

Thomas Jefferson and the other so-called Founding Fathers wrote the Declaration of Independence in 1776, when America broke away from British rule, as a statement of ideals based on equality of opportunity for all. One hundred and fifty years later, Fitzgerald depicts a society divided along lines of social class. The Buchanans and other residents of East Egg live in houses that resemble palaces. The Wilsons, working people, live above their garage in the bleak 'valley of ashes' (p. 26).

STUDY FOCUS: WEALTH A04

Inherited wealth means that some can live luxuriously without effort, while poor people struggle to survive. *The Great Gatsby* shows how this social inequality leads some individuals (Wolfshiem, and Gatsby himself) to engage in serious crime. Myrtle Wilson becomes Tom's mistress in order to spend some time in a world of wealth and glamour that is otherwise closed to her.

A PEACE-LOVING NATION

Jefferson envisaged America as an agrarian society, based on farming and living from the land. But the census of 1920 showed that America had become a predominantly urban nation for the first time. Most Americans now lived in cities, although in reality some of these so-called cities were actually fairly small towns. Note that Jay Gatsby rejects the farming lifestyle of his parents, and after living on Dan Cody's yacht he heads for the city.

Thomas Jefferson also envisaged America as a peace-loving nation. He saw that European societies had been badly damaged by wars, and hoped that America could avoid the waste of human lives in such conflicts. But Fitzgerald stresses the significance to his characters of the First World War (1914–18). In April 1917, America was drawn into this major European conflict. Both Nick and Gatsby served in France, in the American army. Gatsby was promoted to the rank of major, and that enhanced his social status once the war was over.

CONTEXT A04

Thomas Jefferson (1743–1826), a remarkable man who became the third president of the United States (1801–09), was actually a slave owner, like many of his contemporaries amongst the American ruling class. He advocated equal opportunities for all, yet still regarded some human beings as his property. From the start, it seems, American ideals were not always reflected in the conduct of daily life.

America had already experienced the turmoil of Civil War, between 1861 and 1865. The soldiers of the Union (also known as the North) fought against soldiers of the Confederacy (the South) over issues including the continued use of slaves by plantation owners in the South. The North eventually won and slavery in America came to an end. But over 600,000 soldiers died, and the American ideal of living peacefully suffered a major blow.

INDIVIDUALISM

America has traditionally cherished the notion of individuals being able to live with minimal interference or regulation from the government. In the view of Thomas Jefferson, 'That government is best which governs least.'

The Great Gatsby portrays an American society in which individuals have recently been drafted into the Army to go to war, and then subjected to Prohibition laws during peacetime. We are told that as a young officer, Jay Gatsby 'was liable at the whim of an impersonal government to be blown anywhere about the world' (p. 142). More generally the novel shows the emergence of a mass-media society in which the individual may be influenced, often without knowing it, by the power of advertising and fashion, spread through cinema, radio and magazines. Individuality becomes a complex issue in such a society.

Are you really in control of your own identity if you are what you wear, or if you are defined by the car you drive or the house in which you live? Does Fitzgerald suggest that young James Gatz, roaming the shore of Lake Superior, had more integrity as an individual than Jay Gatsby, living with an image borrowed from the European upper class, wearing imported clothes and driving a British car?

REVISION FOCUS: TASK 8   A04

How far do you agree with the statements below?

- Jay Gatsby *is* America.
- *The Great Gatsby* portrays the reality of American society as a betrayal of American ideals.

Try writing opening paragraphs for essays based on these discussion points. Set out your arguments clearly.

KEY QUOTATIONS: AMERICAN IDEALS   A01

Key quotation 1: 'His parents were shiftless and unsuccessful farm people – his imagination never really accepted them as his parents at all' (p. 95).

Possible interpretations:

- Gatsby's imagination enables him to conceive alternatives to the life he was born into.
- America values shifted in the early twentieth century from rural life to urban existence.
- Gatsby is prepared to isolate himself from his own family in order to pursue his own goals as an individual.

Key quotation 2: 'a fresh, green breast of the new world' (p. 171).

Possible interpretations:

- America offered a 'green', natural alternative to European civilisation.
- America offered nurture to new arrivals, as a mother does to her child.
- America seemed a land of 'fresh' opportunity and endless potential.

CONTEXT   A04

The American individualist and philosopher Henry David Thoreau (1817–62) went further than Jefferson; he suggested 'That government is best which governs not at all'. In his influential book *Walden* (1854), Thoreau advocated a simple and self-sufficient way of life. He felt that human beings needed to shed material possessions on the way to finding spiritual fulfilment. The extravagant lifestyles depicted in *The Great Gatsby* are far removed from Thoreau's ideal.

THE AMERICAN DREAM

A MATTER OF INFINITE HOPE

The American Dream is a very familiar phrase, but what does it actually mean? In its most positive sense, the American Dream means that in this land of opportunities, anything is possible and anyone can be a success, no matter what their background. When Nick Carraway refers to Gatsby's 'extraordinary gift for hope' (p. 8), we are being encouraged to recognise Gatsby as an embodiment of the American Dream.

SELF-IMPROVEMENT

A closely related version of the American Dream has a more practical side; it suggests that if you work hard and live an honest and respectable life, you are bound to improve your position in the world. This is the American Dream that is reflected in the schedule drawn up by young James Gatz in his copy of the book *Hopalong Cassidy*. Here, he resolves to rise from bed at 6 a.m., and then at specifically allocated times to study, to work and to improve his way of speaking and his physical posture. He also resolves 'Be better to parents' (p. 164).

GET RICH QUICK

The American Dream has also come to mean simply getting rich quickly. It's that materialistic version of the Dream that Gatsby seems to fulfil when he makes enough money in just three years to buy his huge mansion in West Egg village. We are led to believe that it was not hard work that enabled him to make this lavish purchase, but criminal activity, including bootlegging.

Across the bay, in East Egg, there are houses like palaces that belong to people such as the Buchanans, who have inherited wealth and have not needed to work for material success. George Wilson, on the other hand, who labours daily at his garage, remains poor and lives in the bleak 'valley of ashes' (p. 26). This vast gap between the privileged and the disadvantaged seems a betrayal of the American Dream of equal opportunity for all.

A FRESH START

An important aspect of the American Dream has been the possibility of making a fresh start. Gatsby tries to re-create himself, concealing the past and apparently abandoning his parents. This might suggest a parallel with the way America tried to cast off the past, to break away from European history and Old World values, when the new nation issued its Declaration of Independence in 1776. Does *The Great Gatsby* suggest that new beginnings are really possible? Or does it show that the present and future are shaped by the past?

KEY QUOTATION: THE AMERICAN DREAM   A01

Key quotation: Henry C. Gatz, looking at his son's 'schedule': 'Jimmy was bound to get ahead' (p. 164).

Possible interpretations:

- Henry C. Gatz has remained devoted to his son and is proud of his achievements.
- Gatsby's father retains faith in old-fashioned virtues of hard-work and self-discipline.
- Henry C. Gatz is out of touch with the reality of Jay Gatsby's life.

THE FRONTIER

GO WEST

Near the end of *The Great Gatsby* there is a famous image of Dutch sailors, experiencing a sense of wonder as they encountered for the first time 'a fresh, green breast of the new world' (p. 171). Early settlers from Europe spoke of America as the New World in opposition to the Old World they had left behind.

As the East coast of America became settled, with towns and later cities, Americans continued to move further across the continent, heading West. Despite the presence of Native Americans, who were there long before the Europeans, the West was regarded by these later arrivals as an empty space where it was possible to make a fresh start. The boundary between the settled land and the empty space was known as the Frontier.

In 1893, a history professor named Frederick Jackson Turner (1861–1932) published an essay entitled 'The Significance of the Frontier in American History'. Turner claimed that the Frontier had produced a distinctive American spirit, democratic in a very practical way and relatively free from European influence. The West, he suggested, held the promise of freedom for everyone. It offered the means to live and provided possibilities for personal development.

By the time Turner was writing, settlement had already extended across America and there was no longer a real Frontier. The Frontier, with its distinctive spirit has remained a powerful idea in American culture, however. American space travel, leaving Earth behind, may be seen as a way of opening up another Frontier, and pushing back the boundaries.

THE WEST IN *THE GREAT GATSBY*

Gatsby possesses 'an extraordinary gift for hope' (p. 8), while Nick reserves judgement, and that too is 'a matter of infinite hope' (p. 7). Hope is a quality long associated with the American West and 'I see now that this has been a story of the West, after all,' declares Nick Carraway in Chapter 9 (p. 167). On a literal level, he seems to mean that all the main characters are from the Midwest, the geographical heart of America. None are actually from the West coast, where America meets the Pacific Ocean, although at one point Gatsby claims, untruthfully, to be from San Francisco (see p. 64). Nick has gone East to work in finance, but has returned home to the Midwest to write his book.

The Midwest is presented as a place where you still find basic American values, such as honesty, trust, and even innocence. From his brief appearance in the book, Gatsby's father, Henry C. Gatz, seems to have these qualities, yet in Gatsby's eyes his father is a failure.

Nick prides himself on being honest, but at the end of the book Jordan says she was mistaken when she took Nick to be 'rather an honest, straightforward person' (p. 168). Jordan herself is cynical and a cheat; Daisy at times seems weak and shallow; Tom is violent and bigoted. In what way is this 'a story of the West, after all' we wonder?

CHECK THE BOOK **A03**

Henry Nash Smith's *Virgin Land: The American West as Symbol and Myth* (Harvard University Press, 1974) is a fascinating study of the role the West has played in the way America sees itself. It contains sections on Thomas Jefferson and his ideals, the frontiersman as Western hero and the myth of the New World garden, and analysis of the Frontier offered by American historian Frederick Jackson Turner.

KEY QUOTATION: THE FRONTIER   **A01**

Key quotation: Dan Cody is described as 'the pioneer debauchee, who during one phase of American life brought back to the Eastern seaboard the savage violence of the frontier brothel and saloon' (p. 97).

Possible interpretations:

- Dan Cody had the pioneering spirit that helped to create America.
- Dan Cody led a debauched life, drinking heavily and using brothels.
- Although it signified a fresh start, the Frontier was in reality violent and dangerous.

DESIRE AND WONDER

'UNUTTERABLE VISIONS'

Gatsby's greatness, for Nick, seems to reside in his capacity for hope and the persistence of his desire. Daisy is the immediate object of that desire, but Nick says Gatsby's hunger for the possibilities that life has to offer 'had gone beyond her, beyond everything' (p. 92).

Nick tells us that to kiss Daisy will not fulfil Gatsby: 'He knew that when he kissed this girl, and forever wed his unutterable visions to her perishable breath' (p. 107). Those 'unutterable visions' are what really motivate Gatsby. It is not so much a specific goal, but Gatsby's intense desire to change the conditions of his own life, his striving to change, that makes him great in Nick's eyes. It is not so much *being* a certain person as having the capacity to *become* someone that matters.

LACK OF PURPOSE

Fitzgerald contrasts the intensity of Gatsby's desire with the cynicism and purposelessness of those around him. Daisy, still in her early twenties, complains that she has 'been everywhere and seen everything and done everything' (p. 22). She cannot imagine that the future holds anything new for her, and the prospect of having to devise ways to spend the years ahead simply appals her. The people she knows also suffer from this lack of purpose. They drift, restless but without direction.

A SENSE OF WONDER

At the end of the novel, Nick writes: 'I thought of Gatsby's wonder when he first picked out the green light at the end of Daisy's dock' (p. 171). Coming immediately after Nick's reference to the Dutch sailor arriving at America's East coast, finding himself 'face to face for the last time in history with something commensurate to his capacity for wonder' (p. 171), Gatsby's sense of wonder might seem trivial. It might indicate the limitations of Gatsby's imagination that he finds a green electric light so awesome. Compared to Daisy's jaded outlook, however, Gatsby's sense of wonder can be seen to bring the world alive for him. His world can still appear enchanted and radiant.

CHECK THE BOOK A03

Tony Tanner's acclaimed study *The Reign of Wonder* (Cambridge University Press, 1965) examines the importance of wonder and naivety in a range of American literary works.

REVISION FOCUS: TASK 9   A02

How far do you agree with the statements below?

- Gatsby desires Daisy because of what she represents rather than who she is.
- Gatsby's visions are necessarily unutterable; they can't be expressed in words.

Try writing opening paragraphs for essays based on these discussion points. Set out your arguments clearly.

KEY QUOTATION: DESIRE AND WONDER   A01

Key quotation: 'the incomparable milk of wonder' (p. 106)

Possible interpretations:

- Wonder suggests childlike innocence.
- Wonder nourishes the imagination.
- This nurturing image is in contrast to the mutilation Myrtle suffers.

VISION AND INSIGHT

A MAKER OF SPECTACLES

Gatsby is a maker of spectacles in the sense that he throws parties that are intended to be seen by Daisy across the bay. The clothes he wears, the cars he drives, the extravagance of his house are all part of the display – all part of the spectacle.

Doctor T. J. Eckleburg is a maker of spectacles in another sense; he makes eye-glasses that correct physical distortions in vision. One of the most striking images in *The Great Gatsby* presents the eyes of T. J. Eckleburg, looming over the 'valley of ashes' (p. 26). This advertising hoarding is a realistic detail from the landscape of 1920s America, but it is also a focal point for the novel's theme of vision, its limits and potential.

At a crucial point in the **narrative**, Michaelis finds his neighbour, George Wilson, staring at the optician's hoarding. Wilson, in a deeply disturbed state following the death of his wife, says, 'God sees everything'. Michaelis tries to correct him, pointing out 'That's an advertisement' (p. 152). But George now sees everything differently. Seeing clearly is not always a straightforward business in this novel.

POINT OF VIEW

Nick Carraway is narrating Gatsby's story as he saw it, but he knows there are other versions which might be told from other points of view. Fitzgerald portrays 1920s America as a world where speculation and gossip spread rapidly, based on partial knowledge. Nick concedes early on that 'life is much more successfully looked at from a single window, after all' (p. 10). Should we agree with that statement? Gatsby, obsessive in his desire for Daisy, seems to look at life 'from a single window', but ultimately that doesn't appear to be a successful way of seeing life. At the end of Chapter 7, Nick leaves Gatsby standing in the moonlight, 'watching over nothing' (p. 139).

A VISIONARY?

Images of sight and seeing occur often in *The Great Gatsby*. Genuine insight is more rare however. Owl Eyes, the visitor to Gatsby's party who wears owl-eyed spectacles, may have the appearance of wisdom conventionally associated with owls, his spectacles may make him look scholarly, but he has in fact been drunk for a week. He is impressed by the realistic effect Gatsby has created in his library, rather than by anything worthwhile that may be learnt there. Owl Eyes appreciates the lengths Gatsby has gone to in projecting his image through spectacles, but he shows no interest in what lies beyond the surface.

Is Jay Gatsby simply a showman? Or are we invited to see him as a visionary, someone who can see beyond what is to what might be? Gatsby fixes his gaze on the green light at the end of Daisy's dock, but through that he sees a host of 'unutterable visions' (p. 107). Is Gatsby a man who deludes himself and tries to hoodwink the world by creating illusions? Or is the capacity to imagine the world differently a true measure of greatness?

KEY QUOTATION: VISION AND INSIGHT A01

Key quotation: 'God sees everything' (p. 152).

Possible interpretations:

- Advertising has taken the place of God in 1920s America.
- In the absence of God, accidents are simply accidents.
- God exists in the novel only for George Wilson, who is deranged following his wife's death.

CODES OF CONDUCT

THE FOUNDATIONS

At the start of his narration, Nick says that after the turbulence of the war he wanted the world 'to be in uniform and at a sort of moral attention forever' (p. 8). He means that he wanted the world to become a disciplined and orderly place, where you knew what was what. Instead, he finds himself in a world filled with uncertainty and unpredictability.

Although he takes pride in his own tolerance, Nick feels the need for some code of conduct to regulate human behaviour (pp. 7–8). In contrast, in Chapter 6, Nick writes about Gatsby's teenage dreams and remarks that Gatsby's 'heart was in a constant turbulent riot' (p. 95). This seems to be just the kind of turmoil that Nick now wants to avoid; he goes on to say that these dreams offered Gatsby 'a promise that the rock of the world was founded securely on a fairy's wing' (p. 96). Gatsby has abandoned the schedule he had earlier drawn up as a guideline for his life. Instead, he is now guided by his imagination.

Would Nick consider that a sufficiently firm foundation for a code of conduct? Note the recurrent use of the word 'founded'. Nick has asserted that 'after a certain point I don't care what it's founded on' (p. 8). Might the 'fairy's wing', the power of imagination, be just as good a foundation for a code of conduct as 'the hard rock' of military discipline?

Fitzgerald develops this theme in various ways. Is it better to live a cautious and disciplined existence, as Nick says he does, or to live passionately, like Gatsby? The former way of life offers security; the latter has intensity, but is dangerous. Nick's **ambivalence** towards Gatsby is really focused on this question of how best to live one's life. At the start he says that Gatsby 'represented everything for which I have an unaffected scorn' (p. 8). Yet he admires Gatsby's capacity to dream, to desire and to hope, and out of respect for that he has written this account of Gatsby's life.

HONESTY IS THE BEST POLICY

In *The Great Gatsby* it seems to be difficult to be honest, even in sport, which depends upon fair behaviour as well as clear codes of conduct. Jordan Baker cheats at golf, and Meyer Wolfshiem fixes the outcome of the baseball World Series. And what of Gatsby's favourite phrase, 'old sport'? It seems to invoke fair play, but in fact it is just an empty affectation.

Nick takes pride in his own honesty. It would be comforting to believe that we are reading an account written by a man we can trust. But can we really trust Nick? Is he being honest about his reasons for admiring Jay Gatsby? Does he honestly believe what he tells us about himself? Remember that near the end Jordan says to him that she believed he was honest, but now realises that she has been mistaken: 'I thought you were rather an honest, straightforward person. I thought it was your secret pride' (p. 168).

> ### CONTEXT — A04
>
> Remember that Thomas Jefferson, Benjamin Franklin and the other early Americans who signed the Declaration of Independence in 1776, breaking away from British rule, are commonly known as the Founding Fathers. America had gone to war in order to become independent, but the foundation of the American republic was an act of imagination, a vision of a new future.

KEY QUOTATION: CODES OF CONDUCT — A01

Key quotation: 'Conduct may be founded on the hard rock or the wet marshes, but after a certain point I don't care what it's founded on' (pp. 7–8).

Possible interpretations:

- After the First World War, Nick craves an orderly life.
- A code of conduct allows you to interpret people's behaviour accurately.
- The outward appearance of a code of conduct is more important to Nick than what lies underneath.

STRUCTURE

LOOKING FOR CLUES

The fact that Nick Carraway is both the **narrator** of *The Great Gatsby* and a character in the story he tells has implications for the structure of the book. Nick's narration essentially involves telling us what he has found out about Jay Gatsby. He also conveys to us his feelings about this man and the events that lead to his death. In doing so, Nick reveals aspects of his own character.

Nick is rather like a detective, finding clues and interpreting them, trying to track down the real Jay Gatsby. In sharing this experience with us, Nick releases information gradually, bit by bit, so we too can have the experience of coming to know Gatsby. All the action of the story has already happened. In part Nick seems to be using the act of narration to make things clearer in his own mind. There remain aspects of Gatsby about which we are uncertain at the end; there are still elements of mystery. A further complication is that while reading his account we may find that we don't fully trust Nick. We are, after all, finding out about him too.

STUDY FOCUS: CLUES — A02

The structure of *The Great Gatsby* involves a trail of clues, some misleading, some helpful. Our task, which is also one of the book's great pleasures, is not just to follow a story but also to decipher the clues. Patterns of words and images emerge and, as careful readers, we need to recognise them and try to discover their meaning.

INTRICATE PATTERNING

The composition of *The Great Gatsby* involves intricate patterns in which certain words, images and events **foreshadow** or echo others. For example, colour words – notably green, white and gold – recur regularly, applied to very different objects. Familiar associations of these colours, such as the association of green with Nature, are modified as the words appear in differing contexts. 'White' is applied to the 'palaces' of the wealthy (p. 11), and to the 'ashen dust' that coats George Wilson's clothes (p. 28). Daisy refers to her 'white girlhood' in the American Midwest (p. 24), which might appear to mean one thing in relation to her white dress (p. 13), but quite another in the context of Tom's remarks on the supposed superiority of the white race (p. 18).

The Great Gatsby is not structured in that straightforward way. Nick Carraway wants us to notice the words: his vocabulary is at times obscure and difficult (words such as 'meretricious', 'postern' and 'orgastic'); his imagery can be elaborate and artificial ('now the orchestra is playing yellow cocktail music', p. 42). Nick is being self-consciously literary and is, in effect, reminding us that he is in the process of becoming a writer as this narrative unfolds. The patterning of the novel reflects not only Nick's activity as a kind of detective, on the trail of Jay Gatsby, but also as a writer, creating *The Great Gatsby*. Nick Carraway has a poetic imagination beneath his prosaic surface.

CONTEXT — A04

The 1920s and 1930s are regarded as 'The Golden Age of Detective' fiction. American writers such as Dashiell Hammett (1894–1961) and Raymond Chandler (1888–1959) worked in this genre during the ten years after *The Great Gatsby* was published. Although Fitzgerald's novel is not detective fiction, it contains some ingredients of that genre: a murder, a suicide, a hit-and-run incident, shady figures from the criminal underworld, a character shrouded in mystery and another (Nick Carraway) who reserves judgement while tracking down the facts.

FORM

THE FIRST-PERSON NARRATOR

The most important literary technique utilised by Fitzgerald in *The Great Gatsby* was recognised immediately by his editor, Maxwell Perkins. Perkins told the author in November 1924 that he felt his book used the most appropriate method for telling the story – a **narrator** who is a participant in that story, but is more a spectator than an actor. This creates a complex **point of view**, which involves us, as readers, in acts of interpretation that necessarily extend to making judgements about Nick Carraway.

STUDY FOCUS: PRESENTING GATSBY   A02

The success of this novel depends heavily upon Fitzgerald's control of how the figure of Jay Gatsby is presented to us. He has to be filtered through Nick Carraway's narration at a suitable pace and with appropriate emphasis to sustain our interest without dispelling the necessary element of mystery. Expressing at the outset his reservations about Gatsby as well as his admiration for him, Nick himself becomes a figure we must interpret. So as we are piecing together the puzzle of Gatsby, we are also modifying our sense of Nick, the man who is telling Gatsby's story.

We experience the immediacy of being addressed by a first-person voice. But we find Nick making carefully formulated and considered comments such as this: 'Instead of rambling, this party had preserved a dignified homogeneity, and assumed to itself the function of representing the staid nobility of the countryside – East Egg condescending to West Egg and carefully on guard against its spectroscopic gaiety' (p. 46).

The narrator has weighed up the situation and lets us share his conclusion in a sentence that is not easy to understand. It is densely written, and uses sophisticated vocabulary. Words such as 'homogeneity', 'staid' and 'spectroscopic' convey that Nick is an educated man; they seem to add weight to a judgement made by a man who is keeping his distance.

THE NARRATOR AS PARTICIPANT

A few pages later we find Nick thoroughly caught up in events: 'I was enjoying myself now. I had taken two finger-bowls of champagne, and the scene had changed before my eyes into something significant, elemental, and profound' (p. 48).

He is still concerned to give us his sense of events, and he is still self-conscious in his use of language, but we are now being addressed by someone sitting in Gatsby's garden, sipping champagne, being part of the action. The form of the novel combines storytelling with interpretation. That interpretation is continuously adjusted, tweaked as Nick sees the events he is describing in a slightly different light.

NARRATIVE PACE

We are given a vivid sense of events taking place, but we are kept aware that Nick is writing his account retrospectively and that act of writing is part of the action of Fitzgerald's novel. *The Great Gatsby* is, essentially, a novel about a man writing a book.

If Fitzgerald had created a narrator who gave away too much detail (or too little) at the wrong time, we would have a very different book. If Nick had placed Jay Gatsby in another light he might have appeared a ridiculously comic figure, a man pathetically in love with a woman unworthy of such devotion. Or he might have appeared an unequivocally sinister character, a shadowy criminal like Meyer Wolfshiem.

As it is, Jay Gatsby, filtered little by little through Nick Carraway's narration, presents an intriguingly complex figure, who is able to carry the weight of associations from American history and myth that Fitzgerald chose to place upon him. The novel's form is largely a result of the way in which Nick's narrative is paced, with a gradual release of vital clues and illuminating information.

DIALOGUE AND THE SCENIC METHOD

VARYING THE VOICE

The story is narrated from Nick Carraway's **point of view**. Fitzgerald must have been acutely aware that this involved potential dangers. For example, Nick's voice might have come to seem monotonous, his manner of expression too self-conscious, or his interest in events too narrow.

Fitzgerald avoids this pitfall by letting Nick, writing his own account of events, give us dramatic exchanges in **dialogue**. Nick mimics the idiosyncrasies of a range of voices. For example, Gatsby's cool delivery and the affectation of his favourite phrase, 'Old Sport'; or Jordan Baker's pointed observations, cynical but often revealing; or Meyer Wolfshiem's stylised Jewish accent.

If Fitzgerald had focused closely on the workings of Nick Carraway's mind, as he mulled over the significance of what he had witnessed, we would probably now have a slow-paced and rather turgid novel. The kind of self-analysis Nick gives us in the opening paragraphs of the book is fine for a few pages, but if sustained for the entire novel, it would make for heavy reading.

SCENIC METHOD

Instead we get a series of dramatic reconstructions. So, in Chapter 2, Nick takes us into the apartment where Tom Buchanan and Myrtle Wilson conduct their extra-marital affair. We hear them talk, and violently squabble as they get drunk. Or in Chapter 4, Nick takes us to a restaurant on New York's Forty-second Street, where we meet Meyer Wolfshiem and discover how close his friendship with Gatsby has actually been.

STUDY FOCUS: READING EVENTS A02

Nick gives us his interpretation of events and characters, but in these dramatic interludes we feel that we are witnessing some of those events first hand, and are actually meeting those characters. The impact is more direct. Yet that means there is scope for disagreement to arise between Nick's conclusions and our own reading of events, especially when he is assessing his own role in the action. Look carefully at the complex relationship between these dramatic set pieces and the commentary supplied by Nick.

In *The Great Gatsby*, each of these scenes is self-contained, yet it echoes or **foreshadows** other parts of the narrative and contains elaborate cross-references. The party in Chapter 2, in Tom and Myrtle's apartment, is paralleled by the party at the Plaza Hotel in Chapter 7. Larger parties are held at Gatsby's mansion, in Chapters 3 and 6. In this way, a formal symmetry is constructed. At the centre of the book, in Chapter 5, Nick and Daisy are reunited over tea at Nick's house.

So Nick's narrative combines his own commentary with lively and varied dramatic scenes that feature skilfully crafted dialogue. The dialogue assists the unfolding of the story. It also serves to develop characterisation, giving us insights into the nature and attitudes of the speakers. We, as readers, are invited to listen in to the conversations, to observe the action and to take note of the body language. Then we may draw our own conclusions.

CHECK THE BOOK A03

Fitzgerald admired the use of this scenic method of narrative construction in the work of American novelist Henry James (1843–1916). Henry James had tried to write plays for the theatre. His efforts were unsuccessful, but he learnt from the experience and began to incorporate dramatic scenes, comparable to those found in stage plays, into his fiction. A good example of his scenic method can be found in the novel *The Spoils of Poynton* (1897), which develops through a series of carefully 'stage-managed' scenes.

CINEMATIC TECHNIQUES

Although we might say that *The Great Gatsby* is essentially a novel about a man writing a book, and although Nick Carraway often uses language in a very self-conscious way, this is also a novel that creates strong visual impressions. Cinema was a relatively new art form when Fitzgerald was writing. It is tempting to view his visual effects, such as the lighting of Gatsby's parties or his striking descriptions of clothing and postures, in cinematic terms.

Remember that films were still silent when Fitzgerald wrote this book; 'talkies' came in a couple of years later. Films were almost exclusively made in black and white, as modern colour techniques were not then available. Editing techniques were far less sophisticated than they are now. But the use of the scenic method, and transitions between one scene and another, gives parts of *The Great Gatsby* a cinematic feel.

Fitzgerald's final novel, *The Last Tycoon* (1941), left unfinished at his death, is set in Hollywood, California. He lived there from 1937, working as a scriptwriter, and died there in 1940. The advent of 'talkies' at the end of the 1920s attracted some serious writers, including John Steinbeck (1902–68) and William Faulkner (1897–1962), to Hollywood, where their skill in scripting dialogue was in great demand and they could make money.

In *The Great Gatsby*, Fitzgerald employs some techniques which might be indebted to the example of the cinema. The most evident is the cut, which he uses to make sudden transitions from one scene to another. Chapter 4 furnishes good examples with the cut from Gatsby's car to a cellar restaurant where he has lunch with Wolfshiem (p. 67), and the cut from that cellar restaurant to the Plaza Hotel where Nick is taking tea with Jordan (p. 72). Chapter 7, in which Myrtle Wilson is killed, relies heavily upon such clean cuts from one scene to another.

In those scenes where small parties occur (at Tom and Myrtle's apartment in Chapter 2 and at the Plaza Hotel in Chapter 7) and in those scenes where large parties are given by Gatsby, we find techniques that can be read in terms of cinematic practice. There are movements, for example, from close-ups to panoramic shots, from focus on an individual character to an overview of the crowd and the setting. Such readings are particularly tempting as Gatsby's house and garden are artificially lit like a film set. Note the care with which Fitzgerald handles lighting effects throughout the novel.

Nick refers to 'the great burst of leaves growing on the trees, just as things grow in fast movies' (p. 9). This comparison between rapidly growing foliage and the action in a speeded-up film shows how attuned Fitzgerald had already become to the new cinematic medium, and the kinds of altered perception it allowed.

CONTEXT · A04

The first film adaptation of *The Great Gatsby* – silent and in black and white – appeared as early as November 1926, just a year and a half after the book's publication in April 1925. It was based upon a play, adapted from Fitzgerald's novel by American dramatist Owen Davis (1874–1956). The play had been presented on Broadway in February 1926. Clearly, the dramatic qualities of *The Great Gatsby* were recognised immediately by Fitzgerald's contemporaries.

REVISION FOCUS: TASK 10 · A02

How far do you agree with the statements below?

● *The Great Gatsby* is essentially a novel about a man writing a book.
● *The Great Gatsby* is a novel that belongs to the age of cinema.

Try writing opening paragraphs for essays based on these discussion points. Set out your arguments clearly.

LANGUAGE

THE WRITTEN WORD

Reading some novels, you are scarcely aware of the words on the page. Instead, it feels as if you are watching the characters and the action directly. But in *The Great Gatsby* we are often made aware of the words. Nick is not always inviting us to look through a transparent window and see what Gatsby is up to; he is writing his own account of Gatsby, and the writing is often what we see.

Sentences such as, 'In his blue gardens men and girls came and went like moths among the whisperings and the champagne and the stars' (p. 41), or 'The moon had risen higher, and floating in the Sound was a triangle of silver scales, trembling a little to the stiff, tinny drip of the banjoes on the lawn' (p. 48), make a vivid appeal to the senses, yet we are still aware of Nick self-consciously at work, trying to introduce poetic concentration into his prose – and succeeding.

VOCABULARY

Nick, educated at Yale University, doesn't shy away from words that might be unfamiliar to many readers. His vocabulary can seem difficult. For example, he suggests that Gatsby has lived in the service of 'a vast, vulgar, and meretricious beauty' (p. 95). The uncommon word 'meretricious' means flashy, or attractive in a shallow way, and it derives from a Latin word for prostitute. Once we understand this, it sheds some light on Gatsby; but before we understand its actual meaning 'meretricious' has already told us that Nick is well-educated and has literary aspirations – he is choosing his words carefully as he writes.

Describing the aftermath of Gatsby's murder, Nick uses some unusual vocabulary: 'adventitious' (meaning accidental), 'pasquinade' (meaning lampoon or parody). He is describing a crime scene, but deliberately steers us away from sensationalism, by making us pause over unfamiliar words. He is putting a brake on our reading, at a moment when we might expect to accelerate.

WORDS IN ACTION

Language communicates meaning, but it can also create special effects within our understanding. Words can do things on the page that make us think differently or in a more complex way. Wolfshiem is said to eat with 'ferocious delicacy' (p. 69). An adjective is coupled with a noun that seems to contradict it, creating an **oxymoron**. This seems to fit with Wolfshiem's character, which is both sentimental and ruthless.

Fitzgerald knew that words, written or spoken, can perform functions that are not simply about carrying meaning. During the encounter between Tom and Gatsby in Chapter 7, we are told that 'The words seemed to bite physically into Gatsby' (p. 126). Tom uses language not just to convey a message, but also to bully. On the next page we find, 'Tom's words suddenly leaned down over Gatsby' (p. 127).

SYMBOLISM

Status symbols feature extensively in the social world of *The Great Gatsby*: a shirt, a car or a house may carry associations of wealth and class. The language in Nick's narrative often carries symbolic associations too. 'Green' is an obvious example of a word that is loaded with symbolic meaning. Green symbolises nature, fertility, growth and lushness in the organic world. But the colour also has other associations: envy or jealousy; immaturity; money – the colour of a dollar bill.

CRITICAL VIEWPOINT A02

The phrase 'ferocious delicacy' (p. 69) may bring to mind Daisy, 'winking ferociously' (p. 18). Later, we find the phrase 'ferocious indifference' (p. 96). On the surface *The Great Gatsby* shows us a world of polite manners and genteel boredom. But the adjective 'ferocious' and adverb 'ferociously', used with nouns and a verb that they don't really fit, reveal an underlying savagery and violence in this society.

CONTEXTS

HISTORICAL BACKGROUND

ADVERTISING AND THE MASS MARKET

America's population more or less doubled in the fifty years before *The Great Gatsby* was published. In order to meet the basic requirements of this growing population, mass-production techniques were developed in factories. In 1913, Henry Ford first used an assembly line to produce his Model-T automobile, but the technique was already well established in the production of other goods for the mass market.

Fitzgerald's novel was written against the background of this rapid growth in consumer products, most of which were standardised – they looked the same and served the same use. Standardisation seemed appropriate to a modern democracy, where all citizens could buy items for their convenience and comfort. Manufacturing companies and large stores based in big cities produced catalogues that enabled Americans living in remote areas to purchase goods by mail order.

The whole notion of advertising changed. Instead of just letting people know what was available, advertisers in the early twentieth century set out to persuade potential customers that they needed to buy a certain product. The techniques of persuasion common in modern advertising started to be developed. Products were given brand names to make them stand out and seem attractive. Packaging became much more important, and salesmen were trained in new marketing techniques.

THE JAZZ AGE

The decade following the First World War in America has become popularly known as the Jazz Age. Jazz start to produce some very fine musicians during the 1920s, such as trumpeter Louis Armstrong (1901–71) and pianist and composer Duke Ellington (1899–1974). But wealthy young white audiences tended to like jazz simply for dancing or as a soundtrack for wild behaviour.

The 1920s were also known at the time as the Golden Twenties or the Roaring Twenties. Fitzgerald portrayed these post-war years as a time of pleasure seeking and indulgence. It was a time when young women, often known as 'flappers', behaved with freedom unknown to their mothers and grandmothers. Many cut their hair short, wore relatively short skirts and used make-up to make themselves more attractive.

GRADE BOOSTER A02

Nick Carraway is narrating in 1924, two years after the events of the story have occurred. Think about the effect this distance has on his narrative. Even only two years on, he is looking back at a time no longer his own.

CHECK THE BOOK A04

An excellent illustrated account of the development of advertising techniques in America during this period is Susan Strasser's book *Satisfaction Guaranteed: The Making of the American Mass Market* (Smithsonian Books, 2004).

CHECK THE BOOK A03

Fitzgerald introduced this newly liberated woman into literature, in short stories such as his early collection *Flappers and Philosophers* (1920).

STUDY FOCUS: SEARCHING FOR PLEASURE A01

In *The Great Gatsby* the search for pleasure continues, notably through parties and drinking. But that search has an air of desperation. Momentary pleasures are soon gone, and for some of the glamorous characters in this novel life seems to have no point at all. Jordan Baker is a good example of a liberated young woman, achieving celebrity as a sportswoman. But her conversation, like that of her slightly older friend Daisy, suggests that she is tired of the world and approaches life with a jaded, cynical outlook.

CONSPICUOUS CONSUMPTION

The term 'conspicuous consumption' was coined by a social scientist named Thorstein Veblen (1857–1929). He was born in the American Midwest in 1857, and published a book in 1899 entitled *The Theory of the Leisure Class*. 'Conspicuous consumption' referred to the way in which some wealthy Americans displayed their wealth through their houses and possessions. Thorstein Veblen was critical of this kind of display, as it often seemed irresponsible, extravagant and wasteful.

The Great Gatsby presents some very obvious illustrations of conspicuous consumption. Tom Buchanan, who is certainly a member of the leisure class, so wealthy that he does not need to work, has a team of polo ponies which he takes with him on his travels. He seems to keep them primarily as a status symbol.

Jay Gatsby has his mansion, lavish parties, cars, motorboats and a new hydroplane. The flamboyance of his lifestyle is remote from the dusty world inhabited by George Wilson. But their worlds collide in the accident that kills Myrtle, and the fact that Gatsby has an expensive and easily identifiable car, a blatant example of conspicuous consumption, seals his fate.

> **CRITICAL VIEWPOINT** A02
>
> In the context of this sense that life has lost its purpose, leaving aimless drifting as the only option, Jay Gatsby's 'extraordinary gift for hope' (p. 8) appears a truly rare quality.

REVISION FOCUS: TASK 11 A04

How far do you agree with the statements below?

- Success, in *The Great Gatsby*, is a matter of money.
- In *The Great Gatsby*, America is a place where style is more important than substance.

Try writing opening paragraphs for essays based on these discussion points. Set out your arguments clearly.

THE FIRST WORLD WAR

The First World War was fought between July 1914 and November 1918. For a few years America refused to take part in the conflict, but in April 1917 the president, Woodrow Wilson, declared that America would join forces with Great Britain, France and their allies against Germany and its allies. Nearly three million men were drafted into the American army and many of them were sent to Europe.

In this novel, Nick Carraway and Jay Gatsby are said to have been amongst those soldiers sent to fight in France. Nick mentions specifically the Battle of the Argonne Forest, an offensive in northern France near the end of the war. The American Army suffered over 100,000 casualties in this battle, which lasted more than a month.

THE LOST GENERATION

Gertrude Stein, a remarkable American writer living in Paris, said that the First World War had produced a Lost Generation. The essence of this Lost Generation is captured brilliantly in *The Sun Also Rises* (1926), by Fitzgerald's close friend, Ernest Hemingway. Hemingway's characters wander aimlessly through Europe, feeling emotionally empty. Fitzgerald had already captured this sense of exhaustion and pointlessness when he wrote, at the end of his first novel *This Side of Paradise* (1920), of a new generation 'grown up to find all Gods dead, all wars fought, all faiths in man shaken'.

PROHIBITION AND ORGANISED CRIME

There is a lot of alcohol consumed in *The Great Gatsby*. Yet it is set during a time when the manufacture and distribution of alcoholic drinks were prohibited in America. This Prohibition commenced on 16 January 1920. Prohibition, championed by the Anti-Saloon League, was intended to raise the nation's moral standards, but to a large extent it had the opposite effect. It was difficult to enforce, as Fitzgerald's novel makes very clear.

It has been estimated that in 1925 there were around one hundred thousand speakeasies – illegal drinking dens – in New York City alone. Bootlegging, the illicit production and supply of alcohol, made rapid fortunes for criminals such as the gangster Al Capone. Bootlegging appears to be a major source of Gatsby's wealth. Prohibition was eventually repealed in 1933.

Organised crime, run by powerful gangsters, was a violent reality in American cities such as New York and Chicago during the 1920s. Actual criminals such as Al Capone, 'Lucky' Luciano, Dutch Schultz and 'Legs' Diamond provided models for the popular gangster movies of the 1930s such as *Little Caesar* (1930), *Public Enemy* (1931) and *Scarface* (1932). Their celebrity did not conceal the fact that these were ruthless and extremely dangerous men.

In *The Great Gatsby* the criminal underworld is represented by Meyer Wolfshiem, a character based on the real-life gambler Arnold Rothstein.

MASS SOCIETY

In 1920, the national census showed that America was, for the first time, a predominantly urban nation, with more people living in cities than in the countryside. Some of the places classified as cities were actually fairly small towns, but nonetheless the trend towards an urban America was unmistakable.

The growth of population due to immigration from Europe, and the movement of African Americans from the South, where their families had in been held in slavery until the Civil War, encouraged this rapid expansion of America's cities.

PHOTOGRAPHY

Photographs of a crude kind were produced as far back as the 1820s. But photography improved from the late 1880s, not least because of innovations made by a young American bank clerk called George Eastman (1854–1932). He patented a new camera, using convenient strips of film rather than bulky plates, and coined the trademark Kodak. A craze for taking photographs soon followed, and in the 1920s photography was a popular hobby.

Some photos appeared in newspapers, magazines and advertisements during the 1920s, and played a role in that decade's involvement with image, glamour and celebrity. But the technology for photojournalism as we know it today didn't really develop until the 1930s.

STUDY FOCUS: PHOTOGRAPHS   A02

Note the role of photographs in *The Great Gatsby*. McKee shows Nick pictures he has taken. Myrtle hangs a photo of her mother on Tom's apartment wall. Gatsby carries a photo from his time at Oxford, and has a picture of Dan Cody on his wall. Henry C. Gatz carries a photo of Gatsby's mansion.

CONTEXT   A04

Thomas Alva Edison (1847–1931), American inventor of the gramophone and the electric light bulb, also invented the motion picture camera.

THE CINEMA

Since the early twentieth century, the American film industry has largely been based on the West coast, in and around Hollywood, California. At the time *The Great Gatsby* was written, films were still silent and in black and white, but they were nonetheless an extremely popular form of entertainment. The first film with sound, *The Jazz Singer*, was released in 1927, and a new era in cinema history began. Fitzgerald spent some time, later in his life, writing movie scripts in Hollywood. He died there, leaving an unfinished novel, *The Last Tycoon*, about a film producer.

Jay Gatsby has the glamour of a movie star. That appearance is enhanced by the way his house and garden are lit. An actual movie director is present at Gatsby's party in Chapter 6, along with a female star, who is described as 'a gorgeous, scarcely human orchid of a woman' (p. 101).

AMUSEMENT PARKS

Amusement parks were the precursors of modern theme parks and usually featured all the attractions of the fun fair. They were extremely popular in America between the beginning of the twentieth century and the end of the 1920s, when a major downturn in the economy led to their decline. Steeplechase Park and Luna Park, located at Coney Island, New York, which is mentioned in *The Great Gatsby*, were still attracting vast crowds.

LITERARY BACKGROUND

Fitzgerald published his first novel, *This Side of Paradise*, in 1920. His second, *The Beautiful and the Damned*, followed in 1922. By the time *The Great Gatsby* appeared, in 1925, he had become a much more skilful and controlled writer.

JOSEPH CONRAD

Fitzgerald himself acknowledged that he had learnt a lot about **narrative** technique from reading the work of Polish-born, British novelist Joseph Conrad (1857–1924). Many of Conrad's books read like tales of adventure, and especially of life at sea; but Joseph Conrad saw the novel as a very serious art form, capable of responding to the complexity of the modern world. Joseph Conrad's novella *Heart of Darkness* (1902) and his novel *Lord Jim* (1900) had a notable influence upon Fitzgerald.

Joseph Conrad believed that there should be no word or phrase in a novel that does not contribute to its overall meaning. You can easily see from its intricate patterning that Fitzgerald shared Conrad's belief while he was writing *The Great Gatsby*. That concentration of meaning, with no wasted words, makes it a far more impressive novel than either *This Side of Paradise* or *The Beautiful and the Damned*.

Fitzgerald followed the practice of Joseph Conrad, in *Lord Jim* (1900) and in *Heart of Darkness* (1902), of making his **narrator** a participant in the story. As readers, we need to pay careful attention to the character of this narrator. We can't simply accept that he is giving us the truth in a detached and reliable way. Nick Carraway is deeply involved in the story he is telling, and in some respects he is an unreliable narrator.

HENRY JAMES

This important technical issue of narrative **point of view** was explored with great sophistication by Joseph Conrad's older friend, the American-born British novelist Henry James (1843–1916). Fitzgerald was also influenced by the scenic method he found in novels by Henry James, where a series of carefully constructed dramatic scenes with **dialogue** is embedded in the narrative, so that we almost feel we are watching a play (or a film) unfold.

The scenic method was also used in novels by Henry James's American friend, Edith Wharton. Fitzgerald sent her a copy of *The Great Gatsby*, and Edith Wharton said she thought his book was a masterly achievement.

CONTEXT   A04

T. S. Eliot's challenging poem *The Waste Land* was first published in 1922. Its form, juxtaposing disparate fragments, resembles the collage forms used extensively in the visual arts during the early twentieth century.

T. S. ELIOT

A number of critics have suggested that *The Great Gatsby* is indebted to T. S. Eliot's poem *The Waste Land* (1922). The debt seems to be more in terms of its portrayal of the 'valley of ashes' (p. 26) as a physically and spiritually desolate landscape, than a borrowing of technique or form. Fitzgerald did send a copy of the novel to T. S. Eliot, inscribed to the 'Greatest of Living Poets'.

THE 'INTERNATIONAL THEME'

T. S. Eliot (1888–1965), like Henry James, was an American who chose to live in England and acquired British nationality. Henry James actually made the comparison of Old World and New World cultures the central theme of his many novels and stories. He called it the 'international theme'. Fitzgerald picks up that theme in *The Great Gatsby*, weighing American against European values.

CRITICAL DEBATES

F. Scott Fitzgerald's reputation

When F. Scott Fitzgerald died in 1940, his reputation as a writer was low. Obituaries tended to characterise him as an author who had failed to fulfil his early promise. He was working in Hollywood, as a scriptwriter, and had become an alcoholic. Some commentators suggested that his drinking problem corresponded to flaws in his later writing.

In fact, early criticism tended to view Fitzgerald as the writer of numerous entertaining but rather lightweight stories, written primarily to make money and be published in magazines. The work he himself regarded as his real achievement, notably *The Great Gatsby*, tended to be overlooked.

A little over ten years later, Fitzgerald had become recognised as one of the major writers in the history of American literature. This change in his reputation was initially due to the efforts of literary critic Edmund Wilson (1895–1972), who secured publication in 1941 for *The Last Tycoon*, the novel Fitzgerald left unfinished, and in 1945 for a collection of Fitzgerald's essays, letters and notes entitled *The Crack-Up*.

Reaction on publication

The Great Gatsby received more favourable reviews than any of Fitzgerald's other books. Its positive critical reception was not matched by sales, but he received letters of praise from fellow writers including Gertrude Stein, Willa Cather and Edith Wharton, and from the poet T. S. Eliot, who thought it was the first significant advance in American fiction since Henry James.

Subsequent criticism

In 1945, the critic Lionel Trilling wrote an essay in which he suggested that Gatsby could be taken as a figure who represented America itself. In 1954, this insight was developed by Marius Bewley in another essay, 'Scott Fitzgerald's Criticism of America'.

The appearance of a series of biographies of Fitzgerald has encouraged some works of biographical criticism, in which certain people and events that provided Fitzgerald with raw material for his fiction are identified.

There have also been essays which have suggested literary influences on the writing of *The Great Gatsby*, notably Joseph Conrad's fiction, the poetry of T. S. Eliot and of John Keats, and a range of Christian and pagan myths. Other critics have focused upon Fitzgerald's language, and upon the formal aspects of the novel, especially the role of the narrator.

> **CRITICAL VIEWPOINT** A03
>
> Lois Tyson, in '...next they'll throw everything overboard...': A Feminist Reading of The Great Gatsby', takes as her starting point Tom Buchanan's reaction to his discovery that his wife has apparently taken Gatsby as her lover. She then proceeds to argue that despite its ostensible criticism of Tom's views, *The Great Gatsby* is a novel that actually reinforces a patriarchal standpoint, in part through its representation of women as limited and shallow.

MORE RECENT APPROACHES

A large number of critical books and essays on *The Great Gatsby* have now been published. Yet the novel continues to stimulate analysis. It is written in a rich and concentrated way, and lends itself to critical readings from a wide range of points of view. Literary critics adopt a variety of approaches. Their readings focus on different aspects on the novel, and this can result in radically differing interpretations.

FEMINIST CRITICISM

Feminist criticism has been concerned to reveal how literary works have supported or challenged the assumptions of a male-dominated social order, often called a patriarchal society. There are numerous strands of Feminist criticism, but a basic approach might show us how the lives of characters in *The Great Gatsby* reflect patriarchal values, or suggest alternatives.

Tom Buchanan is clearly an embodiment of those patriarchal values. He likes to exercise power over women, even to treat them as his possessions. When Myrtle upsets him, Tom asserts his authority through violence and breaks her nose. Daisy often seems to have no will of her own and to follow helplessly in Tom's wake. When she does choose to exercise her will, visiting Gatsby's house, Tom gets angry and says, 'Nowadays people begin by sneering at family life and family institutions, and next they'll throw everything overboard and have marriage between black and white' (p. 124).

A Feminist critic might cite this as an example of how the traditional family unit in American society, dominated by the male's powerful role as husband and father, has constrained the lives of women, in their role as loyal wife and mother. In this outburst we can see how Tom's desire to maintain control spills over into overt racism.

A Feminist approach might also point out that Jay Gatsby's obsession with an idealised version of Daisy does nothing to help the actual woman to achieve her liberation. Indeed, Daisy is apparently driven still further into subservience to the domineering Tom Buchanan.

MARXIST CRITICISM

The philosopher Karl Marx (1818–83) suggested that history has involved a long struggle between social classes. He argued that the working class would eventually overthrow the wealthy ruling class, who exercise power and control the way daily life is led in a capitalist society. A Marxist literary critic might focus upon the lives of George and Myrtle Wilson, running a garage in the 'valley of ashes' (p. 26), in order to show how workers were oppressed in America during the 1920s.

The Wilsons are condemned by the economic system to remain poor, and to live in a bleak, unhealthy environment. The wealthy – who never seem to work – live in luxury, in houses that are compared to palaces, and behave like lords in the feudal society of the European Middle Ages. The rich seem to be trying to roll back time, to reverse the history of class struggle and go back to an earlier social order.

A Marxist approach might criticise Jay Gatsby for denying his working-class roots, for using criminal means to enter the ranks of the ruling class and for then behaving like a knight in an old-fashioned **romance**, with Daisy as the grail at the end of his quest. Gatsby's death might be seen, within this perspective, as the inevitable outcome of an individual directing all his energy into a purely personal fantasy, rather than engaging with the kind of social injustice that leaves people such as Tom Buchanan with power and leisure, while working people have to labour and suffer hardship.

CRITICAL VIEWPOINT A03

Lois Tyson, in 'You Are What You Own: A Marxist Reading of *The Great Gatsby*', suggests that while it portrays in a superficially appealing way the glamorous lifestyle of the wealthy, the novel is actually 'a scathing critique of American capitalist culture and the ideology that promotes it'. Tyson argues that Fitzgerald effectively depicts ways in which dedication to commodities (and the process of commodification) in this culture results in dysfunctional interpersonal and social relationships.

PSYCHOANALYTIC CRITICISM

The neurologist Sigmund Freud (1856–1939) developed the discipline of psychoanalysis, which suggests that human behaviour is to a large extent determined by desires and drives of which we are unconscious. We may become aware of these desires and drives through indirect means such as dreams, or slips of the tongue.

A literary critic taking a psychoanalytic approach might point to the passage where we learn that as a boy, Gatsby's 'heart was in a constant, turbulent riot. The most grotesque and fantastic conceits haunted him in his bed at night' (p. 95). In these waking dreams, Gatsby tussles with unconscious desires that he can't really grasp.

The physical realities of his boyhood, growing up on a farm in the Midwest with ordinary parents, didn't live up to the power of these desires, so Gatsby left his parents and severed contact with them. By erasing his parents in this way, Gatsby was psychologically releasing himself to be born again. Meeting Daisy, he was introduced to a previously unknown way of life that in certain ways matched his unconscious desires. His obsession with Daisy became a means to bring into existence the person he himself longed to be.

Nick tells us that Gatsby 'knew that when he kissed this girl, and forever wed his unutterable visions to her perishable breath, his mind would never romp again like the mind of God' (p. 107). In this psychoanalytic reading, then, Daisy is not in herself the object of Gatsby's desire; she is just one more stage prop in his psychic drama. Gatsby's love is actually self-love; he is driven by a powerful unconscious desire to become 'The Great Gatsby'. In his attempt to become this fantasy self, he destroys James Gatz, destroys his parents and eventually destroys Jay Gatsby too.

CRITICAL VIEWPOINT **A03**

Lois Tyson, in '"What's Love Got to Do with It?": A Psychoanalytic Reading of *The Great Gatsby*', views the novel as 'a drama of dysfunctional love'. Her approach focuses upon a fear of intimacy that inhibits relationships between Tom and Daisy, Tom and Myrtle, between the Wilsons, and between Nick and Jordan. The prevailing fear is that the formation of emotional ties to another person will result inevitably in emotional devastation. The novel, seen in this light, is a tense account of unresolved psychological conflicts.

PART SIX: GRADE BOOSTER

ASSESSMENT FOCUS

WHAT ARE YOU BEING ASKED TO FOCUS ON?

The questions or tasks you are set will be based around the four **Assessment Objectives**, **AO1** to **AO4**.

You may get more marks for certain **AOs** than others depending on which unit you're working on. Check with your teacher if you are unsure.

WHAT DO THESE AOS ACTUALLY MEAN?

	ASSESSMENT OBJECTIVES	MEANING?
AO1	Articulate creative, informed and relevant responses to literary texts, using appropriate terminology and concepts, and coherent, accurate written expression.	You write about texts in accurate, clear and precise ways so that what you have to say is clear to the marker. You use literary terms (e.g. '**protagonist**') or refer to concepts (e.g. 'the American Dream') in relevant places.
AO2	Demonstrate detailed critical understanding in analysing the ways in which structure, form and language shape meanings in literary texts.	You show that you understand the specific techniques and methods used by the writer(s) to create the text (e.g. **narrative** voice, **dialogue**, **metaphor**). You can explain clearly how these methods affect the meaning.
AO3	Explore connections and comparisons between different literary texts, informed by interpretations of other readers.	You are able to see relevant links between different texts. You are able to comment on how others (such as critics) view the text.
AO4	Demonstrate understanding of the significance and influence of the contexts in which literary texts are written and received.	You can explain how social, historical, political or personal backgrounds to the texts affected the writer and how the texts were read when they were first published and at different times since.

WHAT DOES THIS MEAN FOR YOUR REVISION?

Depending on the course you are following, you could be asked to:

- Respond to a general question about the text as a whole. For example:

How does F. Scott Fitzgerald tell the story in Chapter 6 of *The Great Gatsby*?

- Respond to a question which challenges you to explore a particular perspective or critical view about the text as a whole: For example:

'*The Great Gatsby* is a novel about cold ambition not love or romance.' Discuss.

- Write about an aspect from *The Great Gatsby* which is also a feature of up to two other texts. This may involve comparison between texts, or require that you write about each in turn. For example:

Discuss the role of the narrator in *The Great Gatsby* and other text(s) you have studied.

TARGETING A HIGH GRADE

It is very important to understand the progression from a lower grade to a high grade. In all cases, it is not enough simply to mention some key points and references – instead, you should explore them in depth, drawing out what is interesting and relevant to the question or issue.

TYPICAL C GRADE FEATURES

	FEATURES	EXAMPLES
A01	You use critical vocabulary accurately, and your arguments make sense, are relevant and focus on the task. You show detailed knowledge of the text.	Nick is both narrator and writer in Chapter 3 as he recollects the events of Gatsby's parties. This means it is from his perspective that the story is told.
A02	You can say how some specific aspects of form, structure and language shape meanings.	Nick's role is also that of a spectator. This has the effect of both distancing the reader so that we can judge what happens, and drawing the reader in.
A03	You consider in detail the connections between texts and also how interpretations of texts differ, with some relevant supporting references.	Nick refers to a family tradition that the Carraways are descended from Scottish dukes. This may remind us of John Durbeyfield, in Hardy's "Tess of the d'Urbervilles" finding out that he has upper class ancestors. Americans are supposed to have left such Old World distinctions of social rank behind.
A04	You can write about a range of contextual factors and make some specific and detailed links between these and the task or text.	The idea of 'the frontier' – the pioneering spirit – is important in the novel, but Nick goes East rather than West, the opposite way to the pioneers.

TYPICAL FEATURES OF AN A OR A* RESPONSE

	FEATURES	EXAMPLES
A01	You use appropriate critical vocabulary and a technically fluent style. Your arguments are well structured, coherent and always relevant, with a very sharp focus on task.	Multiple perspectives are always suggested in "The Great Gatsby", even if they are not the lens through which the story is told. Indeed, Tom's view of Gatsby is integral both to the narrative action and to the way we see both men.
A02	You explore and analyse key aspects of form, structure and language and evaluate perceptively how they shape meanings.	The narrative, as it is filtered for us by Nick's eyes, moves from the immediate – for example, in the dialogue about Daisy's bruised finger in Chapter 1 – to a more distant overview in which Nick draws conclusions, for example saying, 'It [the evening] was sharply different from the West ...' In this way, we are constantly switching focus from the close-up to the long-shot.
A03	You show a detailed and perceptive understanding of issues raised through connections between texts and can consider different interpretations with a sharp evaluation of their strengths and weaknesses. You have a range of excellent supportive references.	A feminist perspective might argue that the women in "The Great Gatsby" are essentially passive. Daisy says, 'I've been everywhere and seen everything and done everything', but this indicates her boredom rather than her active agency in the novel. She has become 'objectified', and is little more than a possession of husband Tom. Elizabeth Bennet, in "Pride and Prejudice" defines herself in terms of her father's status when discussing her relationship with Darcy: 'He is a gentleman; I am a gentleman's daughter; so far we are equal.' But she still shows far more independence of mind and spirit than Daisy Buchanan.
A04	You show deep, detailed and relevant understanding of how contextual factors link to the text or task.	The American Dream and the rise of industrial power which led to increasing wealth towards the end of the nineteenth century and at the beginning of the twentieth are reflected in different ways through Tom and Gatsby – one has real inherited wealth and the other pretends to. Socio-economic factors also affect George Wilson, who lives under the shadow of the increasing gap between the haves and have-nots.

HOW TO WRITE HIGH-QUALITY RESPONSES

The quality of your writing – how you express your ideas – is vital for getting a higher grade, and **AO1** and **AO2** are specifically about **how** you respond.

FIVE KEY AREAS

The quality of your responses can be broken down into **five** key areas.

1. THE STRUCTURE OF YOUR ANSWER / ESSAY

- First, get **straight to the point in your opening paragraph**. Use a sharp, direct first sentence that deals with a key aspect and then follows up with evidence or detailed reference.
- **Put forward an argument or point of view** (you won't **always** be able to challenge or take issue with the essay question, but generally, where you can, you are more likely to write in an interesting way).
- **Signpost your ideas** with connectives and references which help the essay flow.
- **Don't repeat points already made,** not even in the conclusion, unless you have something new to add.

TARGETING A HIGH GRADE · A01

Let's imagine you have been asked about Nick's reliability as a narrator. Here's an example of an opening paragraph that gets straight to the point:

Nick's reliability as a narrator is in question from the start. When he remarks that Gatsby 'represented everything for which I have an unaffected scorn', he not only sets up a critical tension between his judgement and the novel's title, but in making that remark he calls into question his opening assertion that he tends to reserve judgement.

Immediate focus on task and key words, leading to an example from the text

2. USE OF TITLES, NAMES, ETC.

This is a simple, but important, tip to stay on the right side of the examiners.

- Make sure that you spell correctly the titles of the texts, chapters, authors and so on. Present them correctly too, with double quotation marks and capitals as appropriate. For example, "The Great Gatsby".
- Use the **full title**, unless there is a good reason not to (e.g. it's very long).
- Use the term 'text' rather than 'book' or 'story'. If you use the word 'story', the examiner may think you mean the plot/action rather than the 'text' as a whole.

3. EFFECTIVE QUOTATIONS

Do not 'bolt on' quotations to the points you make. You will get some marks for including them, but examiners will not find your writing very fluent.

The best quotations are:

- Relevant
- Not too long
- Integrated into your argument/sentence.

TARGETING A HIGH GRADE

Here is an example of a quotation successfully embedded in a sentence:

When Tom Buchanan calls Gatsby 'Mr Nobody from Nowhere', he is implicitly asserting the value and authority of his own social background.

Remember – quotations can be a well-selected set of three or four single words or phrases embedded in a sentence to build a picture or explanation, or they can be longer ones that are explored and picked apart.

4. TECHNIQUES AND TERMINOLOGY

By all means mention literary terms, techniques, conventions, critical theories or people (for example, 'paradox', 'archetype', 'feminism' or 'Plato') **but** make sure that you:

- Understand what they mean
- Are able to link them to what you're saying
- Spell them correctly.

5. GENERAL WRITING SKILLS

Try to write in a way that sounds professional and uses standard English. This does not mean that your writing will lack personality – just that it will be authoritative.

- Avoid colloquial or everyday expressions such as 'got', 'alright', 'ok' and so on.
- Use terms such as 'convey', 'suggest', 'imply', 'infer' to explain the writer's methods.
- Refer to 'we' when discussing the audience/reader.
- Avoid assertions and generalisations; don't just state a general point of view ('Nick Carraway's narration cannot be taken at face value because it is flawed'), but analyse closely with clear evidence and textual detail.

> **EXAMINER'S TIP** ✓
>
> Something examiners pick up is that students confuse 'narrator' and 'author'. Remember that Nick is a character as well as the narrator and don't confuse him with the novel's author F. Scott Fitzgerald.

TARGETING A HIGH GRADE

For example, note the professional approach here:

Fitzgerald conveys the sense of a society struck by a malaise, drifting towards its ruin while the party still goes on. As readers we feel a sense of decay and decadence as the chapter progresses ...

EXAMINER'S TIP ✓

Answer the question set, not the question you'd like to have been asked. Examiners say that often students will be set a question on one character (for example, Nick Carraway) but end up writing almost as much about another (such as Gatsby himself). Or they write about one aspect of the question (for example, 'disillusionment') but ignore another (such as 'moral decay'). **Stick to the question**, and answer **all parts of it**.

CLOSE READING OF SPECIFIC EXTRACTS

Reading and responding to a specific extract or section of the text is an essential part of your study of *The Great Gatsby*. You will be expected to select appropriate information, draw conclusions and make interpretations. When it comes to your exam, you may be asked to focus on a specific part of the text you are studying. For example:

> How does the manner of Nick's narration in the opening pages of Chapter 1 differ from the way he tells us about the party in Tom's apartment in Chapter 2?

It is important that, from your study, you are familiar with:

- **Where** and **when** this passage/chapter occurs **in the text** (is it the ending of a sequence of events or the actual end of a chapter or key section?).
- What is **significant** about the extract in terms of **the writer's methods (AO2)** (for example, whose voice is it related through? How is it structured? etc.).

WRITING AN EXAM RESPONSE

You must comment on the **writer's methods** specifically (**how** Fitzgerald does it).

DO:	DON'T:
• Consider narrative style and structures, for example, not only making Nick Carraway both a participant in the action and the book's narrator, but also presenting him as the writer of the book, self-consciously at work on every page. • Explore Fitzgerald's use of language, for example, the contrast between Nick's reflective commentary, displaying his taste for obscure vocabulary, and the varied use of dialogue, notably in the party scenes. • Think about the importance of setting and how Fitzgerald portrays it as part of the story (where relevant), for example the stark contrast between the 'white palaces' of East Egg and the 'valley of ashes'. • Focus on form, for example, the way that Nick tells his story rather like a narrator in detective fiction, gradually introducing facts he already knows, while sustaining our interest in the mystery surrounding Jay Gatsby.	• Just re-tell the story/plot • Just write about who the characters are and what they do • State what the themes are unless linked to the writer's methods • 'Micro-analyse' – in other words, don't write extensively on just one single word or a particular type of punctuation. This may look impressive, but you need to be sensible about how much real impact those choices the writer makes may have.

There are **two** key things you should do when writing about an extract:

- **Focus** immediately on a specific aspect
- **Develop** your points with detail

For example, in your first paragraph immediately focus on a key aspect of the writer's methods. Don't waste time with general waffle or plot summary.

> *In the opening to this extract, Fitzgerald uses the device of self-conscious first-person narration to make us aware that all the events in this story are filtered through Nick Carraway.*

In your second paragraph introduce further ideas or develop in more detail your first point.

> *This technique is especially important because it invites us actively to interpret not just the life and character of Jay Gatsby, but the life and character of Nick Carraway. This may make the novel far less straightforward than a third-person documentary account, but it produces a narrative that is far more rich in potential meaning.*

In further paragraphs you should aim to cover new methods used by the writer and make links between and across the methods. As a whole, your essay should work towards a clear, precise conclusion that directly answers the question.

RESPONDING TO A GENERAL QUESTION ABOUT THE WHOLE TEXT

Alternatively, you may be asked to write about a specific aspect of *The Great Gatsby* – but as it relates to the **whole text**. For example:

> **What is the significance of narrators in *The Great Gatsby*?**

This means you should:

- Focus on **'narrators' specifically** (not all characters)
- **Explain** their **'significance'** – why they are important, in your opinion
- Look at the **whole text**, not just one chapter or extract

STRUCTURING YOUR RESPONSE

You need a clear, logical plan, as for all tasks that you do. It is impossible to write about every section or part of the text, so you will need to:

- Quickly note 5–6 key points or aspects to build your essay around

  Point a *Nick, the narrator, remembers that Jordan Baker has cheated at golf.*

  Point b *Nick, throughout his narration, prides himself on his honesty.*

  Point c *As his narrative unfolds, there are times when Nick appears untrustworthy.*

  Point d *Nick says that Jordan is 'incurably dishonest', but is still attracted to her, which may make us less willing to trust his judgements as narrator.*

  Point e *Jordan says that she was wrong to think that Nick is honest and straightforward, which may make us doubt his reliability, even though Nick himself is recording Jordan's criticism.*

- Then decide the most effective or logical order. For example, **point b, then** *c, a, d, e,* etc.

You could begin with your key or main idea, with supporting evidence/references, followed by your further points (perhaps two paragraphs for each). For example:

Paragraph 1: first key point: *Nick prides himself on his honesty.*

Paragraph 2: expand out, link into other areas: *This appears to be a particularly valuable quality as so much gossip, rumour and uncertainty surrounds the character of Jay Gatsby.*

Paragraph 3: change direction, introduce new aspect/point: *George Wilson, unhinged by the death of his wife, mistakes an advertising hoarding for the eyes of God and says 'God sees everything'. But in this novel we get only Nick's far more limited point of view, and there are times when we feel we can't trust him.*

And so on.

- For your **conclusion**, use a compelling way to finish, perhaps repeating some or all of the **key words** from the question. For example, you could end with:

Your final point, but **add a last clause** which makes it clear what you think is key to the question: *While we hear other voices throughout the text, such as Jordan's account of Daisy crying on the night before her wedding, it is ultimately Nick's narrative that determines the way we view the action and issues.*

A **new quotation** or an **aspect** that's **slightly different from** your main point: *Early in his narrative Nick says, 'Gatsby turned out all right at the end'. He prepares us from the start for a story that will justify his own interest in Jay Gatsby. At the end of the novel, Gatsby has lost everything, yet Nick has, in a sense, brought him back to life through his writing. We may conclude that through Nick's significant re-making of Gatsby, he has indeed 'turned out all right'.*

Or, of course, you can combine these endings.

> **EXAMINER'S TIP** ✓
>
> You may be asked to discuss other texts you have studied as well as *The Great Gatsby* as part of your response. Once you have completed your response on *The Great Gatsby* you would move on to discuss the same issues in your other two texts. Begin with a simple linking phrase or sentence to launch straight into your first point about your next text, such as:
>
> *'The impact of new technology is also felt in "Tess of the Urbervilles", where steam trains from London not only connect the Vale of Blackmore with the wider world, but also bring in a school teacher from the city, who changes the way Tess speaks her native tongue.'*

QUESTIONS WITH STATEMENTS, QUOTATIONS OR VIEWPOINTS

Another type of question you may come across is one that includes a statement, quotation or viewpoint from another reader. These questions ask you to respond to, or argue for/against, a specific point of view or critical interpretation.

For *The Great Gatsby* these questions will typically be like this:

- **How do you respond to the idea that Gatsby is not in love with Daisy but with what Daisy represents?**
- **'The central idea of *The Great Gatsby* is injustice in all its different forms.' How far do you agree with this statement?**
- **How far do you agree with the idea that the character of Jay Gatsby is presented as heroic?**
- **To what extent do you think that codes of conduct are important to the novel as whole?**

The key thing to remember is that you are being asked to **respond to a critical interpretation** of the text – in other words, to come up with **your own** 'take' on the idea or viewpoint in the task.

KEY SKILLS REQUIRED

The table below provides help and advice on answering the question: **Discuss the assertion that in *The Great Gatsby* the lifestyle of the wealthy is presented as a goal worth striving for.**

SKILL	MEANS?	HOW DO I ACHIEVE THIS?
Consider different interpretations	There will be more than one way of looking at the given question. For example, critics might be divided about F. Scott Fitzgerald's analysis of social class.	• Show you have considered these different interpretations in your answer. For example: *It is true that one might consider the title to imply that Gatsby has achieved greatness through his wealth. Another interpretation is that he is great because his vision carries him beyond the material trappings of success. However, the name "The Great Gatsby" may just point to the fact that he is a showman.*
Write with a clear, personal voice	Your own 'take' on the question is made obvious to the examiner. You are not just repeating other people's ideas, but offering what **you** think.	• Although you may mention different perspectives on the task, you settle on your own view. • Use language that shows careful, but confident, consideration. For example: *Although it has been said that Daisy is a victim of patriarchal oppression I feel that a more fundamental problem is that, when she marries Tom, she allows the values of her social class to overrule her feelings as an individual.*
Construct a coherent argument	The examiner or marker can follow your train of thought so that your own viewpoint is clear to him or her.	• Write in clear paragraphs that deal logically with different aspects of the question. • Support what you say with well-selected and relevant evidence. • Use a range of connectives to help 'signpost' your argument. *We might say that Nick identifies with Gatsby. However, there are significant differences in their material circumstances. Moreover, Nick says in Chapter 1 that Gatsby represented everything for which he felt 'unaffected scorn'.*

ANSWERING A 'VIEWPOINT' QUESTION

Here is an example of a typical question on *The Great Gatsby*:

Consider the argument that Gatsby is not in love with Daisy but with what Daisy represents.

STAGE 1: DECODE THE QUESTION

Underline/highlight the **key words**, and make sure you understand what the statement, quote or viewpoint is saying. In this case the key words are:

- Consider the argument: *think about/reflect on and respond to the statement that...*
- not in love with Daisy: *does not have real, emotional attachment to Daisy*
- what Daisy represents: *what Daisy symbolises or stands for*

The viewpoint/idea expressed is: *Gatsby is not in love with a woman but with a particular lifestyle, or an idealised notion of that lifestyle.*

STAGE 2: DECIDE WHAT YOUR VIEWPOINT IS

Examiners have stated that they tend to reward a strong view which is clearly put. Think about the question – can you take issue with it? Disagreeing strongly can lead to higher marks, provided you have **genuine evidence** to support your point of view. Don't disagree just for the sake of it.

STAGE 3: DECIDE HOW TO STRUCTURE YOUR ANSWER

Pick out the key points you wish to make, and decide on the order that you will present them in. Keep this basic plan to hand while you write your response.

STAGE 4: WRITE YOUR RESPONSE

You could start by expanding on the statement or viewpoint expressed in the question. For example, in **paragraph 1**:

The viewpoint expressed in the question suggests that Gatsby's devotion to Daisy is not really love for a flesh-and-blood woman, but an obsession with the way of life he first encountered through meeting Daisy.

This could help by setting up the various ideas you will choose to explore, argue for/ against, and so on. But do not just repeat what the question says or just say what you are going to do. Get straight to the point. For example:

He has created his own image in such a way that it will appeal to Daisy's taste. When she visits Gatsby's mansion in Chapter 5, Nick remarks that 'he revalued everything in his house according to the measure of response it drew from her well-loved eyes'. But James Gatz had already started to create the Jay Gatsby he has become some years before meeting Daisy Fay. ...

Then proceed to set out the different arguments or perspectives, including your own. This might be done by dealing with specific aspects or elements of the novel one by one. Consider giving 1–2 paragraphs to explore each aspect in turn. Discuss the strengths and weaknesses in each particular point of view. For example:

Paragraph 2: first aspect:

*To answer whether this interpretation is valid, we need to **first of all** look at ...*

It is clear from this that .../a **strength** *of this argument is*

However, I believe this suggests that .../a **weakness** *in this argument is*

Paragraph 3: a new focus or aspect:

Turning our attention to ... it could be said that ...

Paragraphs 4, 5, etc. onwards: develop the argument, building a convincing set of points.

Furthermore, if we look at ...

Last paragraph: end with a clear statement of your view, without simply listing all the points you have made.

EXAMINER'S TIP ✓

Clearly signpost your ideas through a range of connectives and linking phrases, such as 'However' and 'Turning our attention to ...'

EXAMINER'S TIP ✓

You should comment concisely, professionally and thoughtfully and present a range of viewpoints. Try using modal verbs such as 'would', 'could', 'might', 'may' to clarify your own interpretation. For example, *I would argue that to say Jay Gatsby is in love with what Daisy represents is only partly true, as I believe that the root of his obsession is a desire to recapture the moment when they both fell in love, a moment in which he experienced more intense feelings than at any other time in his life.*

COMPARING *THE GREAT GATSBY* WITH OTHER TEXTS

As part of your assessment, you may have to compare *The Great Gatsby* with or link it to other texts you have studied. These may be other novels, plays, or even poetry. You may also have to link or draw in references from texts written by critics.

Linking or comparison questions might be:

> **Compare and contrast the importance of narrators in *The Great Gatsby* and *Small Island*.**

Your task is likely to be on a method, issue, viewpoint or key aspect that is common to *The Great Gatsby* and the other text(s), so you will need to:

> **Evaluate** the issue or statement and have an **open-minded approach**. The best answers suggest meaning**s** and interpretation**s** (plural):
>
> * Do you agree with the statement? Is this aspect more important in one text than in another? Why? How? Is it possible to detach the story of *The Great Gatsby* or *Small Island* from their narrating voices?
> * What are the different ways that this question or aspect can be read or viewed?
> * Can you challenge this viewpoint? If so, what evidence is there? How can you present it in a thoughtful, reflective way?

> Express **original or creative approaches** fluently:
>
> * **Synthesise** your ideas – pull ideas and points together to create something fresh.
> * This is a linking/comparison response, so ensure that you guide your reader through your ideas logically, clearly and with professional language.

> Know **what to compare/contrast**: **form, structure** and **language** will **always** be central to your response, even where you also have to write about characters, contexts or culture:
>
> * Think about: standard versus more conventional narration (use of flashback, foreshadowing, disrupted time or narrative voice which leads to dislocation or difficulty in reading).
> * Consider different characteristic uses of language (lengths of sentences, formal/ informal style, dialect, accent, balance of dialogue and narration; difference between prose treatment of an idea and poem).
> * Look at a variety of symbols, images, motifs (how they represent concerns of author/ time; what they are and how and where they appear; how they link to critical perspectives; their purposes, effects and impact on the narration).
> * Consider aspects of genre (to what extent do Fitzgerald and the author of Text 2/3 conform to/challenge/subvert particular genres or styles of writing?).

WRITING YOUR RESPONSE

The depth and extent of your answer will depend on how much you have to write, but the key will be to **explore in detail**, and **link between ideas and texts**. Let us use the following example:

> **Explore how writers present emotionally intense relationships in *The Great Gatsby* and *Pride and Prejudice*.**

EXAMINER'S TIP ✓

Be sure to give due weight to each text – if there are two texts, this would normally mean giving them equal attention (but check the exact requirements of your task). Where required or suggested by the course you are following, you could try moving fluently between the texts in each paragraph, as an alternative to treating texts separately. This approach can be impressive and will ensure that comparison is central to your response.

EXAMINER'S TIP ✓

To be original or creative you don't need to come up with entirely new ideas, but you need to show that you're actively engaged with thinking about the question, not just reproducing random facts and information you have learned.

INTRODUCTION TO YOUR RESPONSE

- Discuss quickly what 'emotionally intense relationships' means, and how well this applies to your texts.
- Mention in support the key relationships that exist in *The Great Gatsby* and in *Pride and Prejudice*.
- You could begin with a powerful quotation that you use to launch into your response. For example:

> *'I've just heard the most amazing thing', Jordan Baker whispers to Nick Carraway in Chapter 3 of "The Great Gatsby". The 'amazing thing' she has heard is that Jay Gatsby has bought his huge mansion on West Egg simply because he wanted to live across the bay from Daisy Buchanan. Nick suddenly realises that Gatsby's extravagant house, his parties and possessions have a single purpose; they express Gatsby's intense feelings for the girl he fell in love with five years earlier.*

MAIN BODY OF YOUR RESPONSE

- **Point 1**: start with one intense relationship in *The Great Gatsby*: what it implies about society, how Fitzgerald fitted it to the issues of the time, why this was/was not 'interesting' for readers at the time, and readers now. How might we interpret that relationship differently through time? What do the critics say? Are there contextual/cultural factors to consider?
- **Point 2**: now cover a new factor or aspect through comparison or contrast of this relationship with another in Text 2 and/or 3. How is the new relationship(s) in Text 2 presented **differently or similarly** by the writer according to language, form, structures used; why was this done in this way; how does it reflect the writer's interests? What do the critics say? Are there contextual/cultural factors to consider?
- **Points 3, 4, 5, etc.**: address a range of new factors and aspects, for example other 'intense' relationships, **either** within *The Great Gatsby* **or** in both *The Great Gatsby* and Text 2. What different ways do you respond to these (with more empathy, greater criticism, less interest) – and why?

> *Myrtle Wilson has also become attached to Tom Buchanan in a way that is emotionally intense. Her feelings for him are so strong that she has come to despise her husband George, and wants to leave him and marry Tom. But Tom's appeal for Myrtle is primarily his wealth. She says that when they first met, during a train journey, 'he had on a dress suit and patent leather shoes, and I couldn't keep my eyes off him...'. Tom's clothes fascinated her. There is an obvious shallowness to her feelings for him. She wants to escape her current way of life and experience the lifestyle of the rich. This may make us think again about Gatsby's feelings for Daisy, whose lifestyle opens up a comparably new world for him.*

CONCLUSION

- Synthesise elements of what you have said into a final paragraph that fluently, succinctly and inventively leaves the reader/examiner with the sense that you have engaged with this task and the texts.

> *In Georgian England, Jane Austen could start her novel with the declaration that, 'It is a truth universally acknowledged, that a single man in possession of a good fortune, must be in want of a wife'. She could then proceed to trace the development of a relationship that results in the initially unlikely, but ultimately suitable marriage of Elizabeth Bennet and Fitzwilliam Darcy. But in 1920s America, the ideal of upward social mobility had complicated the picture. Tom Buchanan is a man with a good fortune and established family background, who gets a wife. Jay Gatsby also manages to make a good fortune, but his pursuit of Daisy is like trying to clutch a dream. She remains a girl from another social class to his own, and F. Scott Fitzgerald consequently presents us with a tragic love story.*

EXAMINER'S TIP ✓

Be creative with your conclusion! It's the last thing the examiner will read and your chance to make your mark.

USING CRITICAL INTERPRETATIONS AND PERSPECTIVES

THE 'MEANING' OF A TEXT

There are many viewpoints and perspectives on the 'meaning' of *The Great Gatsby*, and examiners will be looking for evidence that you have considered a range of these.

Broadly speaking, these different interpretations might relate to the following considerations:

1. CHARACTER

What **sort/type** of person Gatsby – or another character – is:

- Is the character an 'archetype' (a specific type of character with common features)? The critic Paul A. Scanlon has suggested that Jay Gatsby is presented as a chivalric knight, and that his courtship of Daisy conforms to the conventions of medieval courtly love.

- Does the character personify, symbolise or represent a specific idea or trope? ('the American Dream'?; 'the tragic hero'?)

- Is the character modern, universal, of his/her time, historically accurate, etc.? (For example, can we see aspects of today's celebrities in Gatsby? Does the way he cultivates his image resemble the way pop icons are presented through the media? Is he establishing a brand, as in a modern advertising campaign?)

2. IDEAS AND ISSUES

What the novel tells us about **particular ideas or issues** and how we can interpret these. For example:

- How society is constructed: the American democratic ideal of equality of opportunity is seen to be frustrated in *The Great Gatsby* by the clear divisions of social class that exist in 1920s America.

- The role of men/women: in the years following the First World War, young women in America behaved in a far more liberated way than their mothers, and Jordan Baker is clearly an independent woman. But the relationship between Tom and Daisy reveals that a patriarchal, male-dominated social order is still very much in place.

- Moral and social codes. Nick says he respects disciplined codes of conduct. Yet he writes a book about a man who has made a fortune through criminal means. Tom Buchanan gets moralistic about Daisy's behaviour when he discovers that she has been visiting Gatsby, but his own conduct is deplorable; he has had numerous mistresses.

3. LINKS AND CONTEXTS

To what extent the novel **links with, follows or pre-echoes** other texts and/or ideas. For example

- Gatsby, who views the world with a sense of wonder and is seemingly a man without a past may be regarded as belonging to a tradition of Adam-like figures in American literature, as outlined in R. W. B. Lewis's classic study, *The American Adam*.

Or:

- Holden Caulfield, the narrator of J. D. Salinger's famous novel *The Catcher in the Rye* (1951), who laments a loss of innocence and lack of honesty in American society, says: 'I was crazy about *The Great Gatsby*. Old Gatsby. Old sport. That killed me.'

EXAMINER'S TIP ✓

Make sure you have thoroughly explored the different types of criticism written about *The Great Gatsby*. Critical interpretation of novels can range from reviews and comments written about the text at the time that it was first published through to critical analysis by a modern critic or reader writing today. Bear in mind that views of texts can change over time as values and experiences themselves change, and that criticism can be written for different purposes.

- How its language links to other texts or modes, such as religious works, myth, legend, etc. For example, Daisy is said to be Gatsby's 'grail'. The word links his pursuit of her to the quest for the Holy Grail, undertaken by knights in the legend of King Arthur.

4. DRAMATIC STRUCTURE

How the novel is **constructed** and how Fitzgerald **makes** his narrative:

- Does it follow particular narrative conventions?
- What is the function of specific events, characters, plot devices, locations, etc. in relation to narrative?
- What are the specific moments of tension, conflict, crisis and denouement – and do we agree on what they are?

5. READER RESPONSE

How the novel **works on the reader**, and whether this changes over time and in different contexts:

- How does Fitzgerald **position** the reader? Are we to empathise with, feel distance from, judge and/or evaluate the events and characters?

6. CRITICAL REACTION

And finally, how do different readers view the novel? For example, different critics over time, or different readers in the early 1920s in the US, postmodern and more recent years.

WRITING ABOUT CRITICAL PERSPECTIVES

The important thing to remember is that **you** are a critic too. Your job is to evaluate what a critic or school of criticism has said about the elements above, arrive at your own conclusions, and also express your own ideas.

In essence, you need to: **consider** the views of others, **synthesise** them, then decide on **your perspective**. For example:

EXPLAIN THE VIEWPOINTS

Critical view **A** about idealism:

> A feminist view of "The Great Gatsby" might argue that Gatsby's idealised view of Daisy does nothing to help her as a woman, and in fact compounds the oppressive treatment she experiences in her marriage to the patriarchal Tom Buchanan.

Critical view **B** about idealism:

> A Marxist view of "The Great Gatsby" might argue that Jay Gatsby betrays the interests of his social class by expending all his energy in pursuit of a personal fantasy.

Then synthesise and add your perspective:

> The idea that Gatsby's idealism adds to the oppression of Daisy, as expressed by a feminist critic, could be considered a persuasive argument, and a Marxist critic's view that Gatsby contributes to his own oppression by ignoring social injustice and becoming obsessed with Daisy seems equally valid. However, I feel that Gatsby's 'extraordinary gift for hope' makes him a positive figure in a society that suffers from debilitating cynicism and world-weariness.

CRITICAL VIEWPOINT **A03**

Here are just two examples of different kinds of response to *The Great Gatsby*:

Critic 1 – Marius Bewley, in his essay 'Scott Fitzgerald's Criticism of America' (1954) developed the idea that Jay Gatsby is 'the "**mythic**" embodiment of the American Dream'.

Critic 2 – David Stouk, in his essay 'The Great Gatsby as Pastoral' (1971), considered F. Scott Fitzgerald's work in relation to the literary tradition of **pastoral**.

EXAMINER'S TIP ✓

Note that Lois Tyson, in her book *Critical Theory Today: A User-friendly Guide* second edition (Routledge, 2006), writes about *The Great Gatsby* from Feminist, Marxist, and Psychoanalytic viewpoints. A critic need not feel constrained by a single point of view. It is possible to read this novel, and think about it in fresh ways, without subscribing to a fixed position as a Feminist, Marxist, or Freudian. You may come to understand much more about *The Great Gatsby* when you read it in an unfamiliar light.

ANNOTATED SAMPLE ANSWERS

Below are **extracts** from two sample answers to the same question at different grades. Bear in mind that these are examples only, using just **AO2** – you will need to check the type of question and the weightings given for the four Assessment Objectives when writing your coursework essay or practising for your exam.

> Question: **How does F. Scott Fitzgerald tell the story in Chapter 2 of *The Great Gatsby*?**

CANDIDATE 1

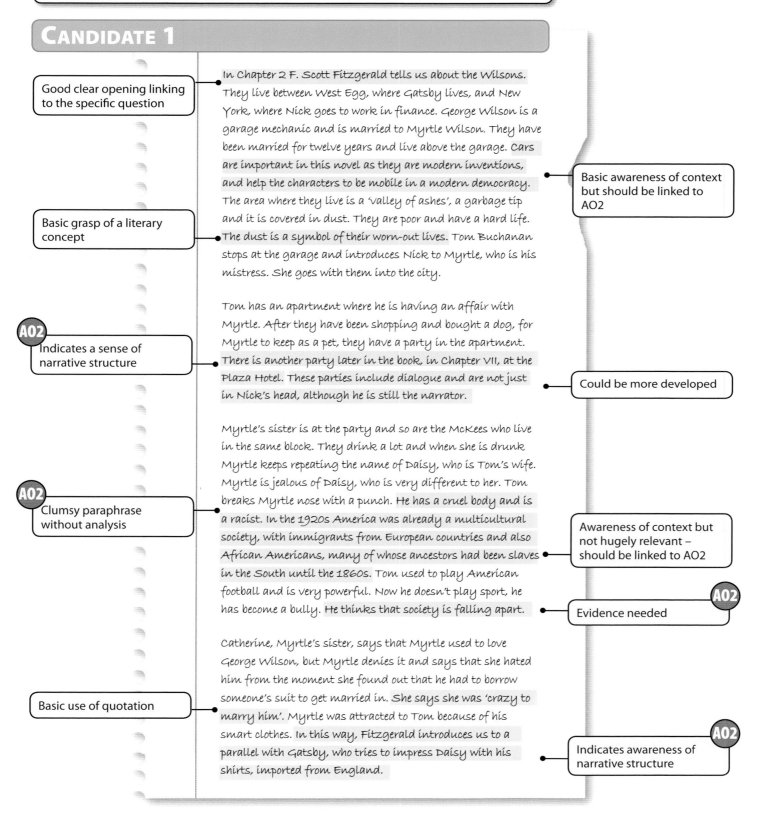

Good clear opening linking to the specific question

In Chapter 2 F. Scott Fitzgerald tells us about the Wilsons. They live between West Egg, where Gatsby lives, and New York, where Nick goes to work in finance. George Wilson is a garage mechanic and is married to Myrtle Wilson. They have been married for twelve years and live above the garage. Cars are important in this novel as they are modern inventions, and help the characters to be mobile in a modern democracy. The area where they live is a 'valley of ashes', a garbage tip and it is covered in dust. They are poor and have a hard life. The dust is a symbol of their worn-out lives. Tom Buchanan stops at the garage and introduces Nick to Myrtle, who is his mistress. She goes with them into the city.

Basic awareness of context but should be linked to AO2

Basic grasp of a literary concept

Tom has an apartment where he is having an affair with Myrtle. After they have been shopping and bought a dog, for Myrtle to keep as a pet, they have a party in the apartment. There is another party later in the book, in Chapter VII, at the Plaza Hotel. These parties include dialogue and are not just in Nick's head, although he is still the narrator.

AO2 Indicates a sense of narrative structure

Could be more developed

Myrtle's sister is at the party and so are the McKees who live in the same block. They drink a lot and when she is drunk Myrtle keeps repeating the name of Daisy, who is Tom's wife. Myrtle is jealous of Daisy, who is very different to her. Tom breaks Myrtle nose with a punch. He has a cruel body and is a racist. In the 1920s America was already a multicultural society, with immigrants from European countries and also African Americans, many of whose ancestors had been slaves in the South until the 1860s. Tom used to play American football and is very powerful. Now he doesn't play sport, he has become a bully. He thinks that society is falling apart.

AO2 Clumsy paraphrase without analysis

Awareness of context but not hugely relevant – should be linked to AO2

AO2 Evidence needed

Catherine, Myrtle's sister, says that Myrtle used to love George Wilson, but Myrtle denies it and says that she hated him from the moment she found out that he had to borrow someone's suit to get married in. She says she was 'crazy to marry him'. Myrtle was attracted to Tom because of his smart clothes. In this way, Fitzgerald introduces us to a parallel with Gatsby, who tries to impress Daisy with his shirts, imported from England.

Basic use of quotation

AO2 Indicates awareness of narrative structure

A02

A point about technique that needs further development

A02

Shows awareness of the tensions that help structure the narrative

One way Fitzgerald reveals the story is through Nick's lack of speech. He doesn't say much during the party and is a quiet person who tends to be more of an onlooker and says at the start of the book that he is 'inclined to reserve all judgements'. Despite this he does make quite a few judgements, such as saying that Jordan Baker is dishonest. Also, despite being quiet he has a love affair with Jordan, even though he still writes to his former girlfriend in the Midwest. Nick gets on with Myrtle's sister and with the McKees, which also shows that although he is quiet he makes friends easily enough and they trust him enough to share secrets with him.

Nick knew Tom at university but this is the first time he has met Myrtle. She doesn't say much to Nick, as she is mainly thinking about Tom and his marriage to Daisy. She wants Tom to get a divorce and run away with her. She shows no real love for George.

A02

Style too matter of fact; not enough analysis of technique

GRADE C

Comment

This answer includes basic information from Chapter 2, but it doesn't really offer a coherent interpretation of events, or address **how** this episode is actually told. There is some understanding of the nature of the characters involved, some insight into their behaviour, but the analysis is fragmentary and could have been developed much more fully and incisively.

The most important omission is a sense that Nick is narrating this chapter. The candidate has shown some awareness of the kind of character Nick is, but has left out the crucial detail that all the action in *The Great Gatsby* is filtered through him. Greater analysis of language, as well as of structure and form needed for AO2.

For a B grade

● Show awareness that Nick Carraway is narrating the story.

● Plan the answer to allow more coherent and connected interpretation, especially of language.

● Make more pointed references to other episodes and elements in the novel as a whole.

● Indicate a firmer grasp of relationships amongst the characters.

● Aim for a more fluent style – try linking sentences.

CANDIDATE 2

Clear and purposeful opening, already engaging with the text

The eyes of Doctor T. J. Eckleburg loom over the 'valley of ashes', which is the initial setting for Chapter 2. Near the end of the novel, George Wilson, a mechanic who runs a garage in this desolate spot, will mistake these eyes, which are actually an advertising hoarding, for the all-seeing eyes of God. In The Great Gatsby there is, however, no god-like overview; rather the story is told from the point of view of the narrator Nick Carraway. The descriptions of places and people in this chapter are all filtered through Nick's understanding. Even when he is not openly commenting upon the action, we need to be aware that his narrating voice is guiding us through events.

AO2 Firm and well-illustrated grasp of structure

AO2 Quotation/evidence needed

Fitzgerald's opening paragraphs of the chapter offer us Nick's description of this bleak area, where New York disposes of its waste. Everything is covered in dust; it looks old and tired. This is in stark contrast to the villages of West and East Egg, whose wealthy residents live in palatial homes. We are told Nick lives in West Egg and commutes to work in the financial district of Lower Manhattan. George Wilson, however, lives over the garage where he works every day. He has been there since he married Myrtle twelve years earlier.

Purposeful use of context linked to AO2

AO2 Point could be expanded

Tom Buchanan, who was at Yale with Nick, introduces him to Myrtle, who is his mistress. Nick is actually a distant relative of Daisy, Tom's wife, but Tom shows no qualms about letting Nick witness his marital infidelity. He actually says 'I want you to meet my girl'. Tom seems to feel that he owns this woman, despite the fact she is married to George Wilson. Tom is very wealthy and makes assumptions that seem more suitable for an Old World aristocrat than a modern American citizen.

Focused use of quotation

Good use of context i.e. related to character development (AO2)

Fitzgerald then shifts the location of the narrative to an apartment in the city where Tom and Myrtle conduct their extra-marital affair. Nick accompanies them and recreates the scene using dialogue as well as description and occasional commentary. Although the dialogue mostly seems trivial is does give us some further insight into the characters involved.

AO2 Good grasp of narrative technique and use of literary terms

Myrtle's dissatisfaction with the conditions of her life become very clear. She regards George as a failure. It is possibly Fitzgerald's intention at this point to bring to the reader's mind the recollection of young James Gatz's perception that his parents were failures. In this way, the author juxtaposes

AO2 Intelligent speculation regarding structuring of narrative

AO2 Awareness of structural parallels

AO2 Awareness of functional use of language

AO2 Grasp of narrative structuring and the use of motif

AO2 A sophisticated and well-expressed point, showing real insight into narrative structuring

AO2 Very well written conclusion, making a link between a 'melancholy scene' and a key aspect of the narrator's character

both relationships: Myrtle sees George as stuck in a rut; James Gatz saw his parents in the same light and left them behind. Myrtle wants to start a new life with Tom. But Fitzgerald's use of dialogue here indicates that that won't happen. Tom is using her, and when he breaks her nose that seems consistent with his attitude towards Myrtle, as well as confirming what we know of his violent and physically powerful nature.

The dialogue also tells us that Myrtle was dismayed to learn that George Wilson had borrowed the suit in which he married her. This may seem a trivial detail for Fitzgerald to reveal, but clothes are an important indication of status in this novel, and in a later scene Daisy responds emotionally to the beauty of Gatsby's shirts, imported from England. The novel is intricately patterned and seemingly insignificant details can take on unexpected meaning.

Myrtle has hung a photo of her mother on the wall of the apartment. This may bring to mind the picture of Dan Cody that Gatsby has on his wall, or the photo of his son's house that Henry C. Gatz carries. Photos freeze a moment in time and that is thematically relevant to Jay Gatsby's attempt to recapture a fleeting moment when he fell in love with Daisy.

Fitzgerald chooses to end the chapter with Nick alone at 4 a.m., waiting for a train to take him home to West Egg. It is a melancholy scene, a man alone at a railway station in the middle of the night. But that fits with the image of himself Nick likes to present, or the one Fitzgerald offers us, at least – a man who feels the sadness of life – that's the man who is our narrator in this chapter and throughout The Great Gatsby.

GRADE A

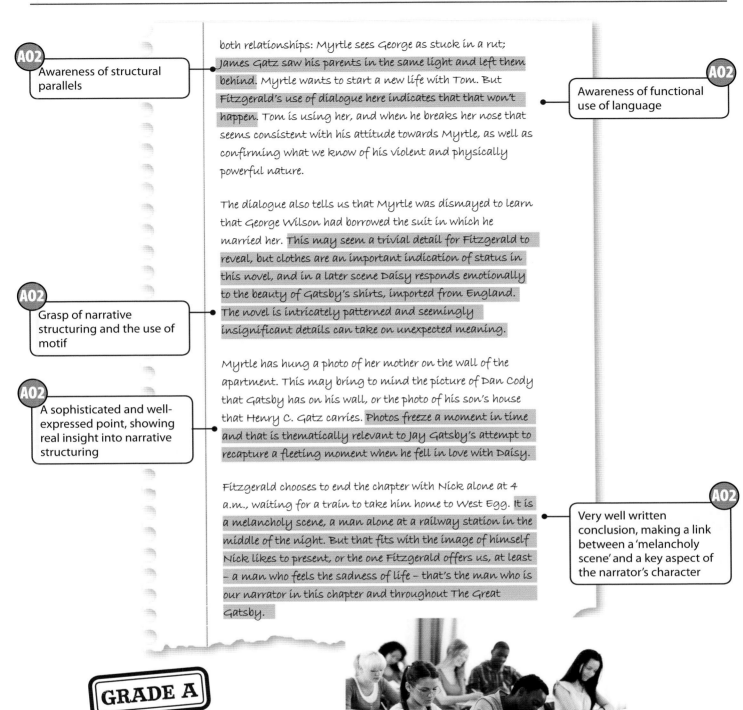

Comment
This is a measured answer – there has clearly been preparatory thought here, and the candidate has structured the essay to make a series of perceptive and relevant points.

A sound grasp is shown of way the novel is structured through intricate patterning of words, images and action (AO2). The use in this episode of incidental details to make narrative links is appreciated (AO2). Those details are also shown to shed light on the social context of America in the 1920s, and to show how Fitzgerald creates character. Importantly, contextual information is linked to AO2 here.

To improve this answer
- Make sure an even greater range of well-chosen quotations is used.
- Make brief yet relevant reference to other literary works.
- Reference and explore a particular critic's point of view in relation to Tom's patriarchal attitudes.

WORKING THROUGH A TASK

Now it's your turn to work through a task on *The Great Gatsby*. The key is to:

- Read/decode the task/question
- Plan your points – then expand and link your points
- Draft your answer

TASK TITLE

> How do you respond to the view that there is only disillusionment and decay in *The Great Gatsby*?

DECODE THE QUESTION: KEY WORDS

How do you respond ...?   = what are **my** views

disillusionment   = hopes and dreams left in ruins

decay   = things/ideas dying and rotting

PLAN AND EXPAND

- **Key aspect: evidence of disillusionment?**

POINT	EXPANDED POINT	EVIDENCE
Point a *Daisy returns to Tom, leaving Gatsby alone*	• *Daisy refuses to tell Tom she never loved him* • *Daisy is prepared to allow Gatsby to take the blame for Myrtle's death* • *Daisy is absent from Gatsby's funeral*	'So I walked away and left him standing there in the moonlight – watching over nothing' (p. 139) 'she and Tom had gone away early that afternoon, and taken baggage with them' (p. 156)
Point b *After Gatsby's death Nick finds that the East appears distorted to him*	Different aspects of this point expanded: *You fill in*	Quotations 1–2 *You fill in*
Point c *George Wilson's dream of going West with Myrtle comes to nothing*	Different aspects of this point expanded: *You fill in*	Quotations 1–2 *You fill in*

- **Key aspect: evidence of decay?**

POINT	EXPANDED POINT	EVIDENCE
Point a *You fill in*	Different aspects of this point expanded: *You fill in*	Quotations 1–2 *You fill in*
Point b *You fill in*	Different aspects of this point expanded: *You fill in*	Quotations 1–2 *You fill in*
Point c *You fill in*	Different aspects of this point expanded: *You fill in*	Quotations 1–2 *You fill in*

- Conclusion:

POINT	EXPANDED POINT	EVIDENCE
Key final point or overall view *You fill in*	Draw together and perhaps add a final further point to support your view: *You fill in*	Final quotation to support your view: *You fill in*

Now look back over your draft points and:

- Add further links or connections between the points to develop them further or synthesise what has been said. Remember to incorporate the views of critics, but make sure that the central idea is your own. For example:

> *Critic Arthur Mizener suggested that "The Great Gatsby" presents 'an image of the fate of Western society'. Although there may be some truth in this, I think Lionel Trilling's argument that Jay Gatsby embodies the fate of America is far more compelling.*

- Decide an order for your points/paragraphs – some may now be linked/connected and therefore **not** in the order of the table above.

DRAFT

Now draft your essay. If you're really stuck you can use the opening paragraph below to get you started.

> *The eyes of Doctor T. J. Eckleberg, staring blankly across the 'valley of ashes' are both a realistic detail from a decade in which advertising played a very important role in American life and a highly charged symbolic image. The unseeing eyes come to represent a failure of the vision upon which America was initially built. The desolate landscape that extends around the advert is literally a waste dump for New York city, but symbolically it is a powerful image of the disillusionment and decay that exist in place of the 'fresh green breast of the new world' that America once offered.*

Once you've written your essay, turn to page 100 for a mark scheme on this question to see how well you've done.

FURTHER QUESTIONS

1. How would you defend or dismiss the argument that *The Great Gatsby* is a novel about Nick Carraway?

2. Consider the claim that *The Great Gatsby* is more about the story of America than it is about one man's life.

3. '*The Great Gatsby* is a study of various kinds of dishonesty and deception.' Make a case for or against that statement.

4. What reasons are there for describing Nick Carraway's use of language as a mixture of history and poetry?

5. Discuss the contention that F. Scott Fitzgerald portrays American success as America's failure.

6. What does Nick Carraway achieve by telling a straightforward story in a roundabout way?

7. How does a grasp of the geography and history of America add depth to your reading of *The Great Gatsby*?

8. How would you support or contest the claim that James Gatz is a tragic figure, while Jay Gatsby is simply a monument to folly?

ESSENTIAL STUDY TOOLS

FURTHER READING

OTHER WORKS BY F. SCOTT FITZGERALD

This Side of Paradise (1920)

Flappers and Philosophers (1920)

The Beautiful and Damned (1922)

Tales of the Jazz Age (1922)

All the Sad Young Men (1926)

Tender is the Night (1934)

Taps at Reveille (1935)

The Last Tycoon (1941)

The Crack-Up (1945)

The novels and collected short stories of F. Scott Fitzgerald are available in paperback editions published by Penguin Books.

The Letters of F. Scott Fitzgerald, edited by Andrew Turnbull, Penguin, 1968

BIOGRAPHIES

Matthew J. Bruccoli, *Some Sort of Epic Grandeur: The Life of F. Scott Fitzgerald*, University of South Carolina Press, 2002
A highly readable and authoritatively informative biography, which conveys a vivid sense of F. Scott Fitzgerald and his time. Contains photographs

Arthur Mizener, *F. Scott Fitzgerald* (Literary Lives) Thames & Hudson, 1987
An approachable account of Fitzgerald's life and assessment of his achievement, illustrated with contemporary photographs.

GENERAL READING

Andrew Blades, *York Notes Companions: Twentieth-Century American Literature*, York Press and Pearson, 2011

Marcus Cunliffe, *The Literature of the United States*, fourth edition, Penguin, 1986
A reliable guide to the history of American literature, including F. Scott Fitzgerald's place within it

Maldwyn A. Jones, *American Immigration*, University of Chicago Press, 1992
Lively, illustrated history of the process of immigration that created modern America

D. H. Lawrence, *Studies in Classic American Literature*, Penguin, 1977; first published 1923
Published before *The Great Gatsby* and concerned with nineteenth-century literature, but it offers very helpful insights into the nature of American idealism and American materialism

R. W. B. Lewis, *The American Adam: Innocence, Tragedy, and Tradition in the Nineteenth Century*, University of Chicago Press, 1955

This is a classic study of the recurrence of the biblical figure of Adam as a thematic touchstone in nineteenth-century American literature. Lewis shows that Gatsby, F. Scott Fitzgerald's deeply **ironic** Adam, had numerous precursors in American writing

Michael McKeon, ed., *Theory of the Novel: A Historical Approach*, Johns Hopkins University Press, 2000

Leo Marx, *The Machine in the Garden: Technology and the Pastoral Ideal in America*, Oxford University Press, 1964
An informative study of literary responses to technology in light of the widely held view of the America West as an unspoilt garden. Marx includes a brief discussion of *The Great Gatsby*

Henry Nash Smith, *Virgin Land: The American West as Symbol and Myth*, Harvard University Press, 1971
Smith tells how the West acquired profound significance within America's perception of itself

Susan Strasser, *Satisfaction Guaranteed: The Making of the American Mass Market*, Pantheon, 1989
An entertaining and informative history of the emergence of consumerism in America, which contains much that is pertinent to *The Great Gatsby*

Tony Tanner, *The Reign of Wonder*, Cambridge University Press, 1965
A study of 'wonder' as a key quality addressed in American literature throughout its history

Michael Woodiwiss, *Organized Crime, United States of America: Changing Perceptions from Prohibition to the Present Day*, British Association for American Studies Pamphlet 19, 1990
A brief, useful summary of the topic

CRITICAL STUDIES

Ronald Berman, *The Great Gatsby and Modern Times*, University of Illinois Press, 1994
Places the novel in the context of its time and place

Harold Bloom, ed., *Gatsby*, Chelsea House, 1991
A series of provocative and stimulating essays

Jeffrey Louis Decker, 'Gatsby's Pristine Dream: The Diminishment of the Self-Made Man in the Tribal Twenties', *Novel*, Fall 1994, pp. 52–71
An essay which engages critically with issues of race raised by the novel

Morris Dickstein, ed. *Critical Insights: The Great Gatsby* (Salem Press, 2009)
A collection that traces the critical reception of the novel from early reviews, troubled by its perceived immorality, to its current reputation as a literary masterpiece

Scott Donaldson, ed., *Critical Essays on F. Scott Fitzgerald's The Great Gatsby*, G. K. Hall, 1984
An invaluable collection of key documents in the history of criticism of *The Great Gatsby*

Hugh Kenner, *A Homemade World: The American Modernist Writers*, Johns Hopkins University Press, 1989
A discussion of F. Scott Fitzgerald and his contemporaries by a major literary critic

Katie de Koster, ed. *Readings on the Great Gatsby*, Greenhaven Press, 1997
A useful collection of essays from several decades, shedding light on the cultural context as well as literary form

A. Robert Lee, ed., *Scott Fitzgerald: The Promises of Life*, St Martin's Press, 1989
Varied selection of new essays on F. Scott Fitzgerald and his work

Robert E. Long, *The Achieving of The Great Gatsby: F. Scott Fitzgerald, 1920–25* Bucknell University Press, 1979
Primarily a study of literary influences, especially that of Joseph Conrad

Lois Tyson, *Critical Theory Today: A User-Friendly Guide* second edition (Routledge, 2006)
A very accessible introduction to critical approaches. Tyson offers helpful and illuminating Feminist, Marxist and Psychoanalytic readings of *The Great Gatsby*.

LITERARY TERMS

ambivalence   the coexistence in one person of two different attitudes to the same object or wish

dialogue   fictional conversation; words spoken between characters

foreshadow   to give an anticipatory indication, or to hint at what will follow later in the narrative

metaphor   describing one thing as being another. This goes further than a **simile** by merging two objects, for example 'the soldier was a lion in battle'

mythic   belonging to myth, that is to stories that lay claim to truth beyond the influence of historical circumstances

narrative   an account of events and action; or events and action that tell a story

narrator   the voice within a written account or story that communicates the account or story to its readers; most simply, the teller of a tale

oxymoron   a figure of speech which combines two apparently contradictory terms, for example 'a wise fool'

pastoral   originally referring to the life led by shepherds, pastoral is the name given to a literary genre in which a simple way of life is compared favourably with a more complex way of life

point of view   the way in which a narrator positions herself or himself in order to approach the materials forming a narrative and deliver them to readers. Examining the point of view helps us to understand how events are filtered through the narrator

romance   a narrative that departs from the dictates of reality as it is known to common sense in order to evoke a magical world (see the description taken from Nathaniel Hawthorne on p. 44)

simile   a kind of **metaphorical** writing in which one thing is said to be like another thing. Similes always compare two things and contain the words 'like' or 'as'. For example: 'the soldier was like a lion in battle'

TIMELINE

F. SCOTT FITZGERALD'S LIFE	WORLD EVENTS	LITERARY EVENTS
1918 Stationed at Camp Sheridan in Montgomery, Alabama	**1918** First World War ends	
1919 Discharged from the army and starts working for an advertising agency	**1919** Baseball World Series is fixed	
1920 Marries Zelda Sayre Publication of F. Scott Fitzgerald's first novel *This Side of Paradise* Publication of the short-story collection *Flappers and Philosophers*	**1920** Prohibition of alcohol commences in the USA (and continues until 1933) US women are given the right to vote	**1920** Edith Wharton, *The Age of Innocence*
1921 Visits Europe	**1921** Silent movie *The Kid*, starring Charlie Chaplin	
1922 Publication of the novel *The Beautiful and Damned* Publication of the short-story collection *Tales of the Jazz Age*		**1922** T. S. Eliot, *The Waste Land*
1923 Performance of the play *The Vegetable* is not a success Starts work on **The Great Gatsby**		**1923** Joseph Conrad, *The Rover*
1924 Moves to the French Riviera		**1924** Ford Madox Ford, *Some Do Not*
1925 Publication of **The Great Gatsby**		**1925** Theodore Dreiser, *An American Tragedy* John Dos Passos, *Manhattan Transfer*
1926 Publication of the short-story collection *All the Sad Young Men*	**1926** Death of the matinée idol Rudolph Valentino	**1926** Ernest Hemingway, *The Sun Also Rises*
	1927 Charles Lindbergh makes the first solo transatlantic flight	**1927** Sinclair Lewis, *Elmer Gantry*
	1929 The Wall Street Crash – the collapse of the New York stock exchange heralds world economic depression	**1929** Ernest Hemingway, *A Farewell to Arms*
	1930 Work starts on the Empire State Building in New York *Little Caesar*, a gangster movie, appears	
1934 Publication of *Tender is the Night*		
1941 *The Last Tycoon* published posthumously		

REVISION FOCUS TASK ANSWERS

TASK 1

Nick Carraway is an unreliable narrator.

- Nick presents himself as a rather dull, reserved individual yet he often uses language in a self-consciously poetic way.
- We have to ask why Nick is so attracted to the glamorous and mysterious Jay Gatsby, especially as he knows of his criminal connections.
- Nick's relationship with Jordan is far from straightforward, and eventually she calls his honesty into question.

In *The Great Gatsby* America is portrayed as a society in love with the European past.

- The wealthy residents of East and West Egg live in houses that are like European mansions, or even palaces.
- Jay Gatsby creates an image of success through items imported from Europe or imitative of European models.
- Although America is a modern democracy, a sense of social class and inequality is pervasive in this novel.

TASK 2

Gatsby's wild parties reflect the turmoil in his heart as he yearns to be with Daisy.

- Gatsby's parties are drunken and indulgent events, typical of the Jazz Age, but he chooses to remain a sober and detached host, at least in the way he appears to onlookers.
- Gatsby generally appears to be a cool and self-possessed character, but when he is with Daisy he behaves, as Nick notes, like an embarrassed boy.
- Appearances in this novel are often deceptive, and we soon learn that despite his calm exterior Gatsby has for a long time been driven by a turbulent inner life.

Fitzgerald portrays America as a land of broken promises and shattered dreams.

- The hopes embodied in 'the fresh, green breast of the new world' (p. 171) have been superseded by the disappointments embodied in the 'valley of ashes' (p. 26).
- Success in the New World is measured in material terms, rather than according to ideals.
- James Gatz's invention of Jay Gatsby in accordance with an ideal vision of himself is comparable to the new beginning that America itself once represented. But Gatsby achieves social success only through illegal activity.

TASK 3

Jordan Baker is a more honest character than Jay Gatsby.

- Jordan is said to have cheated in a golf tournament; Gatsby is said to have become wealthy through bootlegging. Neither is a model of honest behaviour.
- Gatsby has 'an extraordinary gift for hope' (p. 8), while Jordan is cynical and world-weary, but is hope or cynicism a more honest reaction to the world they live in?
- Gatsby takes Nick at face value, whereas Jordan eventually sees Nick as dishonest, and she is disappointed by that.

America is presented in this novel as a land of delusion and injustice.

- George Wilson and Henry C. Gatz are both down-to-earth working men, and both are presented as failures.

- Tom Buchanan's privileged family background determines his wealthy lifestyle, whereas both Gatsby and Meyer Wolfshiem resort to crime in order to get rich.
- George Wilson utters the words, 'God sees everything' (p. 152), but he is actually looking at an advertising hoarding, and George then murders Gatsby in the mistaken belief that he drove the car that killed Myrtle.

TASK 4

Daisy is not worthy of Gatsby's love.

- Daisy married Tom Buchanan, a wealthy and powerful man, rather than waiting for Jay Gatsby to return from the war in Europe.
- Daisy seems a shallow character, drifting through life without purpose, even though she has a small daughter.
- But we need to ask whether anyone could be worthy of Gatsby's love, given its unrealistic basis.

Jay Gatsby is not worthy of the epithet 'Great'.

- The title of the novel tells us that Gatsby is 'great', and that may be Nick Carraway's perception of him, but we don't see any real evidence to support that view.
- Gatsby is successful in terms of being wealthy, but that wealth was achieved by corrupt and criminal means.
- Gatsby's possessions may suggest that he is 'great', but ultimately they are nothing more than the theatrical props of a showman.

TASK 5

Crime is made to seem glamorous in this novel.

- Nick is fascinated by Gatsby's glamorous lifestyle but that has been achieved and sustained through crime.
- Honest labour, of the kind represented by George Wilson, is seen to result only in a bleak and dust-covered lifestyle.
- Meyer Wolfshiem is, however, unmistakably a sinister character.

Nick often uses language in a way that is too self-consciously literary.

- Nick's unassuming character, as he himself describes it, often seems at odds with his self-consciously poetic use of language.
- Nick's decorative language can make sinister events and characters seem acceptable.
- But it can be argued that it is only through self-conscious literary prose that Nick can do justice to the story he is telling.

TASK 6

Daisy's character is revealed through the way she behaves with her daughter Pammy.

- Fitzgerald uses images such as 'the pap of life' (p. 107) and 'the fresh, green breast of the new world' (p. 171) to suggest the nurturing nature of maternal care, but Daisy seems devoid of motherly instinct.
- Daisy says the best thing a girl can be in this world is 'a beautiful little fool' (p. 22).
- Apart from echoing Tom's racist views, Daisy shows no concern for the future of the society in which her daughter will grow up.

Tom's character is revealed through his response to Gatsby's love for his wife Daisy.

- Tom has a mistress, and it is suggested that he has had a series of earlier affairs.
- Ignoring his own behaviour, Tom is shocked to recognise that a love affair between Daisy and Gatsby might be possible.

- Tom reacts not only by disparaging Gatsby's social class, but also by suggesting that an unfaithful wife is another indication that society as a whole is in decline, with other races posing a major threat.

TASK 7

Jay Gatsby was 'great' because he stood apart from the crowd.

- In a modern democracy, such as America, the notion of greatness raises complex issues. In a mass society, such as America, the relationship of the individual to the crowd raises complex issues.
- Nick presents Gatsby as a special person, but key aspects of his character may be seen to correspond to American society as a whole.
- Gatsby's 'greatness' may be that he embodies American values and characteristics. But the novel does call into question whether American society actually has the qualities of 'greatness'.

The presence of Henry C. Gatz makes Jay Gatsby seem more human.

- The pride in his son that Henry C. Gatz displays has an honesty that is rarely encountered elsewhere in this novel.
- Gatz reveals that his son has had some contact with him during the preceding years, and that makes Gatsby seem less selfish, less driven by a single idea, less of an image and more of a man.
- Gatz embodies Midwestern values that seem out of place in the East, and that sheds light on the Midwestern values residing behind Gatsby's new and flashy identity.

TASK 8

Jay Gatsby *is* America.

- Gatsby, like America, makes a conscious break with the past and makes a fresh start.
- Gatsby grows up on a farm, but ends up in a city. That seems to reflect the broad current of American history, which by 1920 had become a predominantly urban nation.
- Gatsby, like America, is driven by an ideal vision, yet defines success in material terms that seem to cheapen the dream.

The Great Gatsby portrays the reality of American society as a betrayal of American ideals.

- The Founding Fathers envisaged that America would be a peace-loving nation, but the novel is set in the aftermath of war.
- The Founding Fathers envisaged that America would be an agrarian nation, but Gatsby's farming parents are presented as unsuccessful and success is associated with the materialistic lifestyle of the city.
- The Founding Fathers envisaged that America would be a land of equal opportunity, but society is depicted in *The Great Gatsby* as divided by inequality along lines of class, race and gender.

TASK 9

Gatsby desires Daisy because of what she represents rather than who she is.

- Gatsby was overwhelmed when, as a young soldier, he encountered the privileged lifestyle of Daisy's family.
- Daisy comes to stand for a social milieu that is the opposite of the routine life that Gatsby knew, growing up on his parents' farm in the Midwest.
- Daisy often appears to be a shallow, disloyal, unthinking woman, and the intensity of Gatsby's desire for her clearly exceeds by far what she might be able to offer him as a person.

Gatsby's visions are necessarily unutterable; they can't be expressed in words.

- When Gatsby started to re-invent his life, as a teenager, he knew what he was rejecting but had no clear idea what he was searching for.
- Gatsby's adult life has been dedicated to finding things in the world to which he can attach his dream. These include his house, cars and clothes. Arguably they also include Daisy Fay.
- Nick's narration uses language that helps to suggest the vividness and intensity of Gatsby's desire, but the concluding words of the novel confirm that whatever he sought in life would always elude his grasp and no words can capture that elusive object of desire.

TASK 10

The Great Gatsby is essentially a novel about a man writing a book.

- Nick has returned to the Midwest to write his account of events in the East, and all we learn is filtered through his understanding.
- Nick says he had literary leanings while at Yale, and the way the book is written often seems self-consciously literary.
- At the end of The Great Gatsby, Jay Gatsby is dead and buried and we are left with Nick preparing to return home and write a book about Gatsby. Or is it a book about Nick Carraway?

The Great Gatsby is a novel that belongs to the age of cinema.

- A film star and her producer are amongst the celebrities who attend Gatsby's parties.
- The care Gatsby shows for his image, for the way it is lit and presented to the public, resembles the care shown by a director shooting a film.
- Some of the techniques used by Fitzgerald, including his framing of scenes and the way he suddenly cuts from one situation to another, may perhaps owe a debt to early cinema.

TASK 11

Success, in The Great Gatsby, is a matter of money.

- Gatsby regards the modest lifestyle of his own parents as lack of success, and instead he takes the wealthy Dan Cody and Meyer Wolfshiem as role models.
- Inherited wealth allows a character such as Tom Buchanan to appear socially superior, despite his obviously flawed character.
- Happiness or fulfilment are not seen in this novel to accompany the acquisition of wealth.

In The Great Gatsby, America is a place where style is more important than substance.

- America is represented in this novel as a land of advertising, materialism, money-making and celebrity rather than a society where higher human values are cultivated.
- Apparently sophisticated characters, such as the Buchanans, are seen to lead lives that are essentially empty, thoughtless and lacking in purpose.
- After Gatsby's death we are left asking what really lay behind his carefully cultivated image. Perhaps it was just an empty dream after all.

MARK SCHEME

Use this page to assess your answer to the Worked task, provided on pages 90–1.

Aiming for an A grade? Fulfil all the criteria below and your answer should hit the mark.*

> **How do you respond to the view that there is only disillusionment and decay in *The Great Gatsby*?**

A01 Articulate creative, informed and relevant responses to literary texts, using appropriate terminology and concepts, and coherent, accurate written expression.

- You make a range of clear, relevant points about remorse, anger and bitterness.
- You write a balanced essay covering both positions.
- You use a range of literary terms correctly, e.g. **foreshadowing**, **metaphor**, **Romance**, **oxymoron**, **dialogue**.
- You write a clear introduction, outlining your thesis and provide a clear conclusion.
- You signpost and link your ideas about remorse, anger and bitterness.

A02 Demonstrate detailed critical understanding in analysing the ways in which structure, form and language shape meanings in literary texts.

- You explain the techniques and methods Fitzgerald uses to present disillusionment and decay and link them to main themes of the text.
- You may discuss, for example, the way that Tom's youthful success on the football field has soured into racist views and violent, sexist behaviour; the cynicism of Jordan Baker, still in her early twenties, or Nick's melancholy and pessimism as he approaches the age of thirty.
- You explain in detail how your examples affect meaning, e.g. Nick's emphasis on Gatsby's 'extraordinary gift for hope' as a positive value makes us acutely aware of the cynicism, pessimism and sense of loss we find in other characters in the novel.
- You may explore how the setting – the houses of the elite on East and West Egg or the bleak 'valley of ashes' – contributes to the presentation of the decay of American ideals and personal disillusionment.

A03 Explore connections and comparisons between different literary texts, informed by interpretations of other readers.

- You make relevant links between decay and disillusionment, noting how they reflect corruption and decline in both the material world and spiritual values.
- When appropriate, you compare decay and disillusionment in the course of *The Great Gatsby* with the presentation of decay and dislliusionment in other text(s), e.g. images of lost innocence, and cosmic blight in *Tess of the d'Urbervilles*.
- You incorporate and comment on critics' views of how decay and disillusionment are presented in the novel.
- You assert your own independent view clearly.

A04 Demonstrate understanding of the significance and influence of the contexts in which literary texts are written and received.

You explain how relevant aspects of social, literary and historical contexts of *The Great Gatsby* are significant when interpreting expressions of decay and disillusionment. For example, you may discuss:

- Literary context: Gatsby takes on a role from chivalric legend, but his fate reflects an irresolvable clash between romance and realism.
- Historical context: Gatsby's route to wealth is connected to Prohibition, and to the violent and lawless underworld of American cities in the 1920s.
- Social context: the decay of American ideals can be seen in the way Tom Buchanan embodies elitism (a society divided along lines of class), sexism (lines of gender), and bigotry (lines of races).

* This mark scheme gives you a broad indication of attainment, but check the specific mark scheme for your paper/task to ensure you know what to focus on.